"You're as bewitchingly seductive as ever."

Rayner groaned the words against her mouth. "I want you and I know you want me. Let's go upstairs."

At his words Marie shuddered back to reality. What was she doing? Her arms slid from around his neck and she pushed him away frantically. Had she learned nothing in all these years?

"I take it that means no," Rayner drawled. "I'm sorry if I offended you, but I have watched you all evening, so cool, serene, the perfect lady. I just had to find out if there was anything left of the young Goldie I once knew." He hesitated and one long finger gently stroked her cheek. "And loved," he said huskily. "I wanted to discover if the passionate girl of my dreams still existed."

Marie blushed—her mind a tumble of conflicting thoughts. Dare she believe him?

JACQUELINE BAIRD hails from Northeast England. She is married and has two sons. She especially enjoys traveling, and has many more ideas stored away for future novels.

Books by Jacqueline Baird

HARLEQUIN PRESENTS
1079—DARK DESIRING
1359—SHATTERED TRUST

Don't miss any of our special offers. Write to us at the following address for information on our newest releases.

Harlequin Reader Service
P.O. Box 1397, Buffalo, NY 14240
Canadian address: P.O. Box 603,
Fort Erie, Ont. L2A 5X3

JACQUELINE BAIRD

passionate betrayal

Harlequin Books

TORONTO • NEW YORK • LONDON
AMSTERDAM • PARIS • SYDNEY • HAMBURG
STOCKHOLM • ATHENS • TOKYO • MILAN

Harlequin Presents first edition February 1992
ISBN 0-373-11431-1

Original hardcover edition published in 1991
by Mills & Boon Limited

PASSIONATE BETRAYAL

CHAPTER ONE

THE small red car raced up the gravelled drive and screeched to a halt at the foot of the massive stone steps that led to the impressive entrance door of the Château Doumerque.

Early September in the Vendée, and the late summer sun shone out of a clear blue sky, turning the grey stones to silver, transforming *'Le Petit Château'*, as it was locally known, into something straight out of a fairy-tale.

The young woman who leapt out of the car, with more haste than elegance, appeared to be immune to the beauty of her surroundings. Dressed as she was in brief white shorts and a T-shirt, her tangled red hair trailed behind her like some medieval banner, her long legs a flash of gold as she took the steps two at a time and disappeared inside the lovely old building.

She was late, very late, but it had been one of those days, she thought, cursing beneath her breath in voluble French. The luncheon party held by one of her grandpapa's employees had turned into a riotous beach party at Les Sables d'Olonne. Not her sort of thing at all, and being half drowned by an over-exuberant eighteen-year-old boy hadn't helped. The final straw had been the puncture on the way home.

'Marie—where have you been? You are late—your grandpapa will be arriving any minute.' The admonishing tone in the brisk demand was obvious.

Marie skidded to a halt on the polished marble floor of the entrance hall, and bestowed her most beguiling

smile on the worried-looking elderly lady blocking her
path.

'I know, Anna, I know... Blame it on a puncture,
and hold the fort until I have a chance to get changed,
please, Anna!' Not waiting for an answer, she deftly side-
stepped around the housekeeper and raced through the
main salon, plus a further couple of reception-rooms,
before she finally reached the foot of the west tower
staircase.

Marie had fallen in love with the château at first sight,
as a nervous seventeen-year-old, and now, seven years
later, she still adored it. It was the only real home she
had ever known, but the exclusion of a central staircase
was a definite drawback, she thought ruefully as, slightly
out of breath, she reached the long gallery on the first
floor. She turned her back on the gallery and quickly
ascended a much narrower spiral staircase to the top of
the tower, and her own private domain.

Years ago, when her mother and Tante Celeste were
girls, Grandmama Doumerque had arranged the reno-
vation of the east and west tower rooms into two self-
contained suites. Marie pushed open the heavy oak door,
and let it slam back behind her. The large, circular room
had been divided in two. The front semicircle was the
bedroom with long windows overlooking the entrance
to the château, and the remaining semicircle was dissected
again to form a small study and a rather elegant, if now
somewhat dated, bathroom.

She crossed her study with a brief glance at her desk,
and opening her bedroom door she sighed with relief;
the sense of peace she felt at reaching her own private
eyrie had a calming effect on her taut nerves. Kicking
off her sandals and stripping off her T-shirt, she hopped
one-legged into the bathroom, trying to remove her
shorts. In seconds she was naked, and shoving her long

hair unceremoniously on top of her head she pulled on a shower-cap and, turning on the shower, stepped gratefully beneath its soothing spray.

Marie hated to be late for anything or anyone; she was a stickler for convention, almost obsessive about it, but with good reason. Her formative years had been spent roaming around England with her French mother and English father—not that she had been allowed to call him Father, he had preferred Tom.

Her parents had delighted in telling her that they had met in Paris in the Sixties. Her mother had been studying at the Sorbonne and her father had been studying art. They had been so wrapped up in their own ideals that they had never recognised how bitterly their young daughter resented their free and easy lifestyle.

Even now, as a mature woman, it still made her blood boil when she saw a television documentary, or read an article, elegising the glorious Sixties. There was never any mention of how the children of these totally self-absorbed parents felt, but she knew from personal experience...

Tom had spent his life fighting authority, and, when he wasn't saving the seals, the white rhino, the whales or the world, he'd preached peace and love for everyone, while as his daughter she would have preferred him to love her, individually, a little more. She had watched her beautiful mother slowly develop an addiction to supposedly harmless drugs. What a joke... All the old resentment churned in her stomach as she remembered her mother, out of touch with reality.

Marie turned off the water and jumped out of the shower. Wrapping a large fluffy towel around her body, she returned to the bedroom, deliberately blanking out the painful memories of the past. From an antique marquetry chest of drawers she extracted lacy briefs and a matching bra, and with a minimum of thought she withdrew a stylish buttercup silk halter-necked dress from an elegant old mahogany wardrobe.

In minutes, she was fully clothed again. She grimaced at her reflection as she sat down at the dressing-table. With a sigh, she picked up a comb and began the tedious task of trying to comb the tangles along with a good deal of sand from her long red hair. Finally she managed to pin it up into some semblance of a chignon, although wayward wisps of curls framed her face and trailed the nape of her neck.

She carefully applied a moisturiser to her lightly tanned skin, a flick of mascara on her long lashes, a touch of lipstick and she was ready. She stood up and tightened the belt of her dress firmly around her narrow waist, unconsciously chewing her lower lip in a nervous gesture. She had felt uneasy ever since her grandpapa's phone call last night, informing her that he was bringing an English guest home. There was no reason for it, but somehow she could not shake the feeling of impending doom.

With a very Gallic shrug of her slender shoulders, Marie told herself to stop being so silly. Her grandpapa had been staying with Tante Celeste and Jacques at their stud farm in Normandy, some twenty miles from Deauville. According to Grandpapa the *haut monde* always went to Deauville late in August. She had been a few times herself and she had to admit he was probably right. The race-track was magnificent and the wealthy and elegant paraded there with more style than any thoroughbred racehorse. It was said Prince Charles in his bachelor days had been a frequent visitor to the town.

The sound of a car arriving interrupted her wayward thoughts, and she crossed to the long window overlooking the forecourt.

Her full lips curved in a fond smile as she watched her aunt and uncle alight from their Range Rover. They were a lovely couple, and their young daughter Janine had been the inspiration for Marie's venture into writing and the subsequent publication of her first children's book. Marie raised her hand to wave, but never completed the gesture as her attention was caught by the two men alighting from the second vehicle, a gleaming metallic grey Jaguar.

Her grandpapa, still a fine figure of a man for all his seventy-odd years, looked remarkably happy, his handsome face covered in a broad grin as he listened appreciatively to something his companion was saying, but it was the other man who caused Marie's fingers to curl convulsively into the velvet window drape, her knuckles gleaming white with the force of her grip.

She stood as though turned to stone, her horrified gaze fixed upon the tall, broad-shouldered stranger. It could not be...she told herself—it must be a trick of the light...

The late afternoon sun cast a silver halo around the man's head as he turned and with a few lithe strides reached the boot of the car and, opening it, withdrew a smart leather suitcase. He straightened to his full height, something over six feet, and with a toss of his proud head, like some predatory animal scenting the air, he strolled to the entrance steps and stopped, a foot on the first step.

She could see his profile clearly, and fear along with a host of other emotions widened her topaz eyes. He turned and looked directly at the tower window. Marie shivered, convinced he had seen her, and worse, much worse... It was Rayner—Rayner Millard...a face from the past.

She staggered backwards, the bed caught the back of her knees, and she sank on to it. She hunched her shoulders, her arms wrapped around her middle in a vain attempt to stop the trembling of her body. The blood drained from her face, the room spun crazily, and her heart seemed to stop beating for long, agonising seconds. She gasped great mouthfuls of air into her starving lungs, and gradually the room stopped spinning to resume its safe familiarity.

Marie had no idea how long she had sat—it could have been seconds, or hours. She only knew that fate, co-incidence, Kismet, whatever, had dealt her a stunning blow. Rayner was here, a guest in her home, and she had to go downstairs and face him...

She jumped off the bed, her movements jerky and un-coordinated. She had no choice. Her grandpapa would expect her to greet his guest, but the thought terrified her. Memories she had banished to the deepest recess of her subconscious mind for years now rose up to haunt her.

She had been just sixteen the first time she had met Rayner. His father had allowed the 'travellers' to camp on his land, and Rayner had appeared to check out the camp-site. To the young Goldie Brown, as she had then been known, he had looked like the white knight of her dreams. He had spoken quite kindly to her, and she fell in love with him on the spot. He'd become the hero of all her youthful fantasies. She had spent the winter dreaming about him—the landowner's son, who would whisk her away from the travelling life she hated, and love her forever.

They had met again the following year, and the reality of him had been much better than her fantasies. He had treated her as a normal person, and listened to her ambition to find a steady job, build a career, and, most important to the young Goldie, live in one place per-manently. On their fourth meeting, she'd gone willingly into his arms, and when his sensuous lips had taken hers in a long passionate kiss, she had responded with all the feverish ardour of a young girl starved of love. Rayner had been a virile young man, and he'd taken everything she had to offer without a qualm. While Goldie had been convinced he loved her...

What a fool she had been. At first she had blamed Rayner, and hated him for the shameful fiasco of their last meeting. But in the years since she had matured. She had long since stopped hating him and accepted the truth. They had just been two young people with an overdose of hormones and a stereotyped image of each other. There was no blame to be apportioned. It was just unfortunate it had ended so disastrously.

Marie shook her head to dispel the disturbing memories, and with a quick stride she crossed the room. A brief glance at her reflection in the cheval-glass restored her confidence. The picture she presented was of a mature woman, simply but elegantly clad in classic silk. She straightened her shoulders, and, with an unconscious gesture, tilted her chin at a proud angle.

She was Marie Doumerque, to her neatly varnished fingertips. A writer and a well-loved member of a fine French family. She had panicked for nothing, she told herself, walking out of the room. There was no way Rayner would recognise the little nobody, Goldie Brown, in the elegant creature descending the stairs.

Marie's lips twisted in a wry smile as she glided through the smaller reception-rooms. It was shock, that was all, that had caused her violent reaction at the sight of Rayner. Her girlish infatuation with him was long since dead, and he was no more likely to remark on their last humiliating encounter in front of her family than fly to the moon...

She was still smiling as she entered the main salon—if anyone was to be embarrassed, it was more likely to be Rayner than her. She had the advantage of knowing whom she was about to meet.

'Marie, *ma petite-fille*, you are well?' Her grandpapa swept her into his arms and kissed her soundly on both cheeks. Then, holding her at arm's length, he scrutinised her from head to toe. 'Anna tells me you have had an accident. I have warned you about driving so fast.'

'Welcome home, Grandpapa, and it was not an accident, just a puncture.' And, shooting a grateful look at Anna, she added, 'I'm fine, and you look wonderful. Your holiday obviously agreed with you.' She realised as she smiled into his gleaming dark eyes that he did look well. For the past few months she had worried about him. A slight heart attack had left him very subdued, but now he seemed to have recovered his old exuberance. With a final brief hug, she turned to greet her aunt and uncle.

In a flurry of embraces, she asked all the usual questions. Marie knew she was overdoing the welcome home bit, but she was strangely reluctant to face the inevitable confrontation with their guest. To her chagrin, she was intensely aware of the tall man standing slightly to one side of the family group, and she was glad of the support of her grandpapa's arm at her elbow as she was introduced to their visitor.

'We are forgetting our guest, child. Monsieur Millard, allow me to present my granddaughter, Marie. Marie, this is Rayner Millard. We met at Jacques's, and he expressed a desire to see something of the west coast of France, so I insisted he stay with us for a few days. I told him I had a beautiful granddaughter who would be delighted to act as his guide, and he couldn't resist my offer.'

Marie felt the colour surge into her face at her grand-papa's words. She had forgotten his deliberate attempts at matchmaking over the past year but this was by far the most embarrassing.

Rayner stepped forward, one strong brown hand extended towards her, and summoning every ounce of self-control she possessed she placed her much smaller hand in his, and raised her head. At least he had not attempted to greet her in the French fashion, and she breathed a sigh of relief. The relief was short-lived as the touch of his hand sent an unexpected jolt of electricity shooting up her arm.

Hastily she withdrew her hand and met his penetrating gaze with barely concealed shock. He was older. Seven years is a long time, she told herself, as she mumured a conventional greeting, but the change in him was incredible.

It was not just the passing of years, she recognised instinctively, as an unwanted pain clutched at her heart. It was more—much more… The blond-haired, laughing, confident young man of twenty-three, whose sparkling eyes had reflected the blue of a midsummer day, was gone, and in his place stood a formidable hawk of a man.

The blond hair was now more silver than blond, and his eyes… They were as grey and hard as flint. The features were the same. The broad forehead and perfectly arched brows, the large straight nose and the square chin, but as for the rest—his sensuous mouth was now a grim straight line, tightly controlled, and there was an addition. A cruel scar curved from the lobe of his right ear across his jaw to the corner of his mouth.

'I am delighted to meet you—Marie... Your grandfather, Henri, has told me so much about you, I feel I know you already.'

There was no answer to that, and Marie did not try to make one. His French was heavily accented, but what he said sent a shiver of fear down her spine. Had his hesitation over her name been deliberate? She didn't know. His 'I feel I know you already' had a decidedly sarcastic edge to it, but his voice—how well she remembered the deep, melodious tone. It had always had the power to excite her, to make her stomach flutter, and to her dismay it still did.

Anger at her own reaction stiffened her spine, and gave her the courage to withstand his cool-eyed assessment of her. His glance travelled with slow deliberation from the red-gold hair piled on the top of her head to her sandalled feet. She felt as if he had stripped her naked, and his seemingly innocent smile did not fool her for a second. She caught the glitter of raw male sexuality in his probing eyes, before his expression relaxed into the bland mask of social politeness.

Hiding behind a cool, haughty exterior, she boldly met his gaze. There was no trace of recognition in his cool grey eyes, just a lingering glimmer of male appreciation. The sort of look he would bestow on any reasonably attractive female at a first meeting.

'You must be tired after your long journey, Monsieur Millard. Please, won't you sit down?' She gestured with a slender hand at a plush velvet sofa, and inwardly breathed a sigh of relief as he seated himself with casual ease next to her grandpapa on the sofa.

She did not know whether to be pleased or insulted that he had not recognised her, but it did dispel her anxiety to some extent. There was no likelihood of his telling her grandfather anything that would upset him.

For that she was grateful, and some of the tension eased out of her and she was able to relax a little.

'Anyone care for a drink?' Jacques asked, crossing the room to where a large selection of bottles stood on the top of an ornate gilt and rosewood cabinet. 'How about you, Rayner? A whisky? You must need one, after driving for hours with Henri as a passenger.'

Marie chuckled and shot an affectionate look at her grandpapa. He was notorious for his back-seat driving— she had suffered from his comments often enough herself.

'No, thank you. I make it a rule never to drink spirits before seven,' Rayner replied easily.

'*Dieu!* You must have a will of iron to stick to that rule,' Jacques opined admiringly.

Marie glanced across at Rayner, who appeared totally relaxed, his long legs stretched out in front of him. He was smiling at Jacques, and for a second she glimpsed the young man she had known. Lowering her lashes to mask her interest, she carefully studied his face and form. His cheekbones were high and slightly prominent, while deep grooves bracketed either side of a stern mouth. His jaw-line jutted hard and square, and the long, slashing scar gave a sinister slant to his features.

Yes, this man did have a will of iron. No one would ever doubt it, Marie thought, shifting uneasily in her seat. Even relaxed, the ripple of muscle was evident beneath the silk knit shirt that covered his broad shoulders and chest. His cream trousers were stretched taut across his hard-muscled thighs. He looked lean, predatory, and all male.

How old was he now? Thirty... thirty-one? She had stuck a year on her age when she had first met him— he might have done the same. She was surprised he was not married, but she knew he could not be, or her grandpapa would never have introduced her the way he had. Whatever, Rayner was still a very sexy man, and he probably had women falling all over him...

She raised her head, and could not stop the tide of colour that swept up her throat and face as her topaz eyes clashed with a pair of sensually aware grey ones. He knew exactly what she had been thinking, she could see it in the glimmer of amusement in the depths of his eyes. Heat flooded her body; she did not hear her grandpapa's laughing disclaimer of his driving habits. Time was suspended as an arc of sexual awareness flashed between them. She forced herself to break the contact, very much aware of her role as hostess.

'Perhaps Monsieur Millard, being an Englishman, would prefer tea,' she offered lightly to somewhere over his left shoulder, privately amazed at the steady timbre of her voice.

'So you remembered,' Rayner drawled slowly, and his gaze slid from the perfect oval of her face down to her breasts and back to her face.

'Remembered what?' she blurted. God! Did he recognise her after all? she thought, tension returning to every line of her body.

'Why, that the British like tea, of course,' he declared blandly. 'Your grandfather told me you were educated in England,' he added by way of explanation.

Marie flicked a glance at her grandpapa. 'Yes, yes, I was.' Why couldn't he have kept his mouth shut? she thought helplessly. God knew what else he had told Rayner. Educated in England, what a joke...

'Whereabouts did you go to school—I might know the area?' Rayner asked.

She was a hopeless liar, and she stuttered, 'W...W...'

'Whitby, in the north of England,' her grandpapa answered for her.

'Yes, the north of England,' she repeated parrot-fashion. The conversation was becoming dangerous, and Marie hadn't a clue what to do about it, but surprisingly Rayner did it for her.

'It must have been hard for you to leave France. You have a beautiful home here,' he commented, with an appreciative look around the room.

To Marie's delight, Aunt Celeste launched into a brief history of the château, so letting her off the hook. She gave a sigh of relief and for the next few minutes allowed the conversation to wash over her.

Slowly she began to relax again, as she looked around the grand salon, trying to see it through the eyes of a stranger. It was a lovely room, dominated by a magnificent marble fireplace. The long windows let in the early evening sun, giving a warm glow to the polished wood of the antique furniture. She loved the ancient Louis XV table with the elegant bowed legs, and the occasional chairs with their softly curved backs. The sofas and soft furnishings were all muted pastel shades, and complemented the mouldings on the walls and ceiling, all exquisitely carved, painted and picked out in gold. Against one wall was one of her favourite pieces, a cabinet in Japanese lacquer that, according to her grandpapa, had come direct from Versailles.

A small smile curved her full lips. She had been silly to panic at Rayner's arrival. There was no way he would connect the daughter of this house with Goldie Brown, the 'hippy'. How she hated that word. She frowned. Even now, it still had the power to hurt...

'Marie will show you to your room, and explain the family portraits as you go. Won't you, Marie?'

Celeste's voice brought her back to the present with a jolt, and, pinning a smile on her face, there was nothing she could do but agree.

She escorted him through the family room. He made the conventional flattering comments about the size and elegance of the château, and remarked on the oddity of the construction as they reached the foot of the west staircase.

Marie was intensely aware of his masculine presence at her side, and her instant reaction to him confused and angered her. Neither by look nor word had Rayner betrayed any hint of recognising Marie. Obviously what had been the most traumatic event of her life had been of absolutely no consequence to him, she thought with a tinge of bitterness she could not quite suppress. But in that she was wrong...

Ascending the stairs, she imagined she could feel the warmth from his body enveloping her as he followed one step behind. She told herself not to be so stupid, but it did not stop the hair on the back of her neck prickling with awareness.

Reaching the gallery, she turned and gave him what she hoped was a confident smile, and with a negligent wave of one hand she indicated a large oak door, some yards along the landing.

'Anna has put you in the blue room.' And with a few quick strides she reached the door and opened it, stepping to one side as she did so. 'I hope you will be comfortable.' With a glance at the fine gold watch on her slender wrist, she added, 'We dine at seven-thirty, so you have over an hour to settle in.' A few more seconds and she would be away from his disturbing presence... But it didn't happen.

'In that case we have plenty of time,' Rayner drawled, but this time in English.

Marie raised startled eyes to his as his hand closed over hers on the doorknob. He pulled the door shut, and somehow she found herself in the bedroom with him.

'Monsieur Millard——' was as far as she got.

'Rayner, please. There is no need to be so formal—after all, we are old friends... Goldie...'

Marie paled beneath her tan, her mouth fell open, and her topaz eyes widened to their fullest extent. For several tense seconds she stared at him in sheer disbelief. Every line on his tanned face expressed a ruthless determination, and she caught a brief glimpse of ferocious rage in the depths of his eyes. She blinked, and thought she must have imagined the anger as his lips quirked in the beginnings of a smile.

'You look like a stranded goldfish,' he opined softly, and raising his hand he pressed one long finger over her still open mouth. 'You were an enchanting young girl, and you have grown into an even more beautiful woman. You could not possibly have believed I would not recognise you. Your face has haunted me for years.'

Her lips tingled where he had touched, and when he dropped his hand to wrap his fingers around her wrist she was too confused to object. He had recognised her... He had not forgotten their previous relationship, brief as it was, and if she could believe his words the memories had haunted him as much as they had her.

'Why—why didn't you say something downstairs?' she asked, finally finding her voice.

'I was waiting for you to acknowledge me; after all, we did part in rather unusual circumstances, and I would hate to have inadvertently embarrassed you by saying something out of line. You appear to have the perfect set-up here—a permanent home and a loving family,' he said smoothly, then added, 'Something you always desired, I seem to recall.'

She eyed Rayner warily—his last comment had sounded decidedly sarcastic. But no, he was smiling down at her, his grey eyes warm and sincere, and once again she saw the young man she had known.

'Yes, well... I think...' She was about to thank him for his consideration, but he did not let her finish.

'And I think you owe me an explanation, Goldie—or Marie—and you can start with your name. I am intrigued how Goldie Brown, the hippy——'

'Not hippy, traveller,' she inserted sharply, and tried to pull her wrist free. He had thrown her off balance with his revelation, but she was beginning to regain her self-control.

To her surprise, he let go of her wrist, and turned his hands palms up in a placating gesture. 'OK, traveller— I know that is the modern-day term for such people. Now will you come and sit down and enlighten me, hmm...?'

Marie meekly allowed him to lead her across the room, and made no resistance when he sat down on the bed and pulled her down beside him. She was frantically trying to gather her scattered wits into some semblance of order. Anger she could have understood, but his reasonable request for an explanation left her feeling strangely perturbed. It was irrational, she knew. They were both mature adults now. What could be more natural than a polite conversation between old friends?

'So, Goldie, how did you become Marie Doumerque, and mistress of a rather lovely château? Please don't keep me in suspense any longer. I know from Henri that you write fairy-tales.' Rayner turned slightly towards her, his grey eyes gleaming with amusement. 'But no fairy-tale could rival the change in your circumstances over the past seven years, I'm sure,' he mocked lightly.

Her full lips curved in a responsive smile. 'No fairy-tale, I can assure you, just the truth.' She frowned; it was not easy for her to say, but if it meant she won

Rayner's confidence and so prevented him from upsetting her grandpapa it was worth it. 'I am a bastard.' There, she had said it . . .

She heard Rayner's quick intake of breath, but she hurried on before he could comment. 'I was born in France, and my parents took me to England when I was a few months old. Oh, they were married after a fashion, the priest a man with flowers in his hair, according to my mother. Unfortunately it was not legal. I was registered as Marigold Doumerque, and I am a French citizen. In England I was known as Goldie Brown. Tom Brown, my father, preferred it.'

'Ah, I remember Tom very well,' he inserted drily.

She threw Rayner a sharp look, disturbed at his tone, but his handsome face showed nothing other than polite concern. She lowered her head and, clasping her hands in her lap, she kept her eyes fixed on them. It was easier than looking at the formidable man beside her, and hesitantly she continued.

'My mother was Michelle Doumerque, Henri's daughter. Seemingly they had a terrible fight when I was just a few months old, and he told her not to return until she was a respectable married woman. I did not know any of this until my mother brought me here, when I was seventeen. She only told me then because I saw my passport. She had applied and got a new one for me, hoping I would go to Turkey with her and Tom, that summer . . .' She paused, and took a deep breath to ease the tension she could feel knotting her stomach. This was the dangerous part. That summer she had known Rayner . . .

'I heard about their deaths. I'm sorry,' Rayner said quietly.

'You heard?' But how could he have known? she wondered.

'Tom had been on television—his death was reported in the English papers. A landslide in Turkey—a tragic accident, they called it.'

'Oh, I see,' she murmured. She did not want to mention her last meeting with Rayner, or her hasty exit from England. 'Anyway, I never went to Turkey. I came here instead,' she said lamely, and raising her head she cast a sidelong glance at Rayner.

'So I see—and I'm glad.' And, catching her glance, he grinned.

Her heart jumped, and deep inside her a tiny flicker of hope took root. Was it possible he would accept her explanation, without raking over the past, and agree to the favour she now had to ask of him?

'You make it sound so simple. Marie and gold, Marigold. I can't think why I didn't work it out for myself.' Rayner laughed, and casually put one arm around her shoulders, drawing her towards him.

The heat of his strong hand on the top of her bare arm seemed to burn through her skin. Marie had to call on all her hard-won self-control to prevent herself pulling away from him. He was only being friendly, she told herself firmly, but she could do nothing about her increased pulse-rate, except hope he did not notice.

'I'm happy for you, Marie, that your parents finally did marry, and Henri took you into his home. You deserved some good luck,' he offered gently.

Marie swallowed hard. 'It wasn't quite like that,' she demurred. 'They never actually married, but when Henri saw my mother again after so many years he forgave her, and he took me in without a qualm.' She hesitated. 'The thing is, Rayner, my mother didn't tell Grandpapa the whole truth about our life in England. She didn't want to cause him any more unnecessary distress, and he is rather a stickler for convention.' She was rambling, but she found it very hard to actually get the words out. She took a deep breath.

'What I am trying to say is that my grandpapa doesn't know we were travellers in England. He thinks we stayed permanently on a farm in Whitby and lived a conventional life, with Tom working at his art in between farming, and I don't want him disillusioned. I love him dearly.' She turned her head to face Rayner, unaware of the pleading gleam in her golden eyes. 'So please, you would be doing me a great favour if you made no mention of our p-past...' She stumbled over the word, not sure how to phrase it, but it didn't matter as Rayner's arm tightened around her shoulder, squeezing gently.

'Don't worry, your secret is safe with me. Henri is a charming man, and your uncle Jacques has agreed to train one of my racehorses, so I expect to have a long and fruitful relationship with your family. The past, as far as I am concerned, is dead and buried,' he assured her emphatically, and dropping his arm from her shoulder he caught her by the hand, and, standing up, pulled her to her feet.

Marie's eyes rounded in pleased astonishment as a wide grin split Rayner's face, and, taking a step back, he made her a sweeping bow. '*Enchanté*, Mademoiselle Doumerque! We meet as strangers, but I hope we will soon become very good friends, *n'est-ce pas*?'

'*Mais oui!*' she responded, unable to suppress a chuckle at his tomfoolery.

'And now for your illustrious ancestors. I don't want Celeste asking me questions I can't answer at dinner...'

If Marie had not been so wound up in her own emotions, elated that it had been so easy, but oddly hurt that he could dismiss their past association so carelessly, she might have noted the mocking cynicism in his last comment and wondered at it. Instead she said, 'Yes, of course,' and turning on her heel she led him back out of the bedroom to the wide hall that doubled as an art gallery. Later, much later, she was to realise that his ready agreement had been too easy...

CHAPTER TWO

'THIS is the art gallery, such as it is. Grandpapa has delusions of grandeur,' Marie informed Rayner with a smile.

'Surely no delusion. I thought he must be a descendant of the crowned heads of France, he has such style,' he said smoothly.

'He would like to think so, but the truth is much more mundane.' Marie loved to look at the old paintings. It gave her such a good feeling of belonging, and enthusiastically she told him, 'The original Henri Doumerque arrived in France by way of Canada, and the California gold fields. Who his antecedents were, nobody knows. He bought a derelict estate, and built this small château, to live the life of a country gentleman.'

'Well, in that case your grandfather could be right. You certainly look very regal, quite a lady,' Rayner drawled softly, his grey eyes darkened as his glance dropped to the full curves of her breasts, down to her small waist, and the soft feminine roundness of her hips, before returning to her face. 'Quite a ... lady.'

Flustered by his searching appraisal, she was horribly conscious of just how well Rayner had known her at one time. She felt the blood rush to her face, wondering if he was remembering the same thing as she was, and she was not at all sure he wasn't mocking her with the word 'lady'. She took a few hasty steps along the hall and stopped in front of a large painting of an elegantly dressed and bewigged man of a bygone age. The artist had captured for all time a roguish gleam in the near black eyes. She took a deep breath and rushed into speech.

'This was the first Henri Doumerque, and it could almost be a portrait of my grandfather, the likeness is stunning. In fact all the Doumerque men were very much alike.' She sounded like a tourist guide, all her former enthusiasm gone—but she didn't care, she just wanted to get it over with so she could escape to her room. She had the awful suspicion that Rayner was just as danger- ous to her emotional well-being now as he had been when she was seventeen. In fact, more so...

'Yes, I can see that,' he agreed, and half turning he flashed her a hard look, adding, 'But what about the women? I would be interested to see if you resemble them.'

This time Marie could not mistake the cynicism in his tone, and with a proud toss of her head she marched on to the next picture. It was the wife of the first Henri Doumerque, a beautiful picture of a red-haired young woman, in an elegant ballgown of the era. 'Colette Doumerque.' Smarting from his implied insult, her tone was curt. 'An Irish American girl the first Henri met and married and brought back to France as his bride.' She stood back and let Rayner examine the painting, knowing what he would see.

'You are the image of this woman. You could have been her twin,' Rayner murmured and, turning, his grey eyes locked with hers. 'There can be no doubt, you are a Doumerque.'

'I never have doubted it,' Marie told him bluntly. 'Now if you will excuse me, I will leave you to study the rest at your leisure.' She glanced at her wristwatch. 'Dinner is served in about half an hour.'

'Marie, thank you, and I apologise for doubting your story.' He must be a mind-reader, she thought wryly.

'Blame it on the cynicism of my old age, and forgive me, please,' he said, a small smile playing around his mouth, his grey eyes glinting down into hers.

She did... Marie doubted if the woman had been born who could refuse Rayner. He was that sort of man, she thought ruefully. The next few days were going to be very difficult.

It was with a feeling of intense relief that she closed her bedroom door behind her. The events of the last couple of hours had left her feeling like a wet rag; sheer will-power and good manners had carried her through, but now she sank down on the bed, the shock finally catching up with her, and if there had been any way of getting out of going down to dinner she would have used it.

She closed her eyes, and took a few deep, calming breaths. She needed to be sensible, and sort out her chaotic thoughts and emotions before facing Rayner again. The fact that he was here at all was the most amazing coincidence—yesterday she would have bet a million to one against ever seeing the man again. In her mind's eye, she pictured his face as they were introduced; he was as handsome as ever, more so. Time, and the scar, had added character and interest to his features and, more than that, he exuded an aura of raw male power that few men possessed.

Marie stirred restlessly on the bed—an elusive thought was tapping at her consciousness. Suddenly it struck her. There had been no shock, no surprise, in Rayner's piercing grey eyes when they had been introduced. Surely that was odd... She sighed. Not really, she told herself ruefully. He was a sophisticated man of the world, well able to hide his emotions. Hadn't he told her the past was dead and buried? God knew, hundreds of women must have passed through his life in the last few years! Why would he be embarrassed by one stupid young girl?

The trouble was, she admitted to herself with bitter honesty, it was no way as easy for her. Memories of the past rose up to haunt her. A wooded glade, lying in Rayner's arms, his tender, almost worshipful kisses on her lips, all over her, and, when he had finally possessed her completely, she had cried out first with pain, and ultimately with ecstasy.

Her body flooded with heat, her breasts hardened beneath the fine silk of her dress, as for a moment she relived the past; then with a groan she rolled over and off the bed, cursing herself for a fool.

She had fought a long, hard battle years ago to forget her night of shame, and now with the arrival of Rayner it had all come back to her. Her emotions had been frozen in limbo for years, and that was how she liked it. She knew her grandpapa thought she was as pure as the driven snow, and oddly enough over the years she had almost convinced herself that the episode with Rayner had been a dream, or nightmare... It was amazing how the human mind could delude itself, she thought sadly, and crossing to the dressing-table she sat down, and studied her reflection in the mirror.

Marie had devoted all her energy for years to her career and home, to the exclusion of everything else. She had had boyfriends—no... Being brutally honest with herself, she had been out on an odd date with a man. A few kisses, and that was the sum total of her experience in the past seven years.

She considered herself a reasonably sophisticated career woman. So who was this person staring back at her from the mirror? she thought with dismay. The topaz eyes gleamed golden, the oval face, flushed and somehow softer, looked invitingly sensuous. She grimaced to dispel the image, but in her heart she knew that seeing Rayner again had reawakened her latent sexuality. In his presence she was intensely aware of him, as she never had been with any other man, and it frightened her.

Mechanically she began repairing her make-up. There was no need to change—the buttercup silk was appropriate for dinner, and she did not want Rayner to think she was trying to attract his attention.

With a brief glance at her watch, she stood up, and ran her hands lightly over her hips, smoothing the soft silk. She straightened her shoulders, and with supreme self-control turned towards the door, her cool, sophisticated image once more intact. Perhaps if Rayner stuck to their earlier bargain his stay might be quite pleasant, she told herself, with more confidence than she actually felt. After all, he had agreed to keep their former association a secret. She walked briskly downstairs. He need not have done that, so obviously he was a reasonable man, and with this consoling thought she entered the dining-room.

Marie's steps faltered, and stopped just inside the room as the first person she noticed was Rayner. He was leaning negligently against the massive green marble fireplace, one elbow resting against the mantelpiece, and in his other hand he loosely held a fluted crystal glass of sparkling amber liquid. It was the first time she had ever seen him dressed in anything other than casual wear, and the shock took her breath away.

His dark dinner-jacket fitted perfectly across his broad shoulders. Where one leg was bent so his elegantly shod foot could rest easily on the ornate brass fender, the fabric of his trousers pulled taut across a muscular thigh. Hastily she raised her eyes, to where the pristine white shirt and complementary silk tie contrasted starkly with the light golden tan of his face. She had always thought him handsome, but tonight he was devastating. Wryly, she acknowledged that his tomfoolery earlier about meeting as strangers held more than a grain of truth. This magnificent male animal was a stranger to her.

He looked up and caught her watching him. Immediately his firm lips parted in a knowing, sensual smile. 'Marie, you look charming,' he drawled mockingly, and his eyes raked her feminine curves with a blatant sexual thoroughness that shocked her rigid.

Marie could feel the heat spreading through her body at his scrutiny, and she was humiliatingly aware he had done it deliberately. He had read her mind yet again, and was playing tit for tat. She swallowed nervously, looking away. Why was it he had this disastrous effect on her? No other man ever had. With a wry grimace she walked across the room, and pulling out the nearest chair she sat down at the table. Her murmured 'thank you', a polite response to his compliment, went unnoticed amid the general conversation.

Much to her surprise, the meal did not turn out to be the ordeal she had expected. Rayner sat next to Marie, and Uncle Jacques and Aunt Celeste sat opposite with Henri at the head of the table.

Anna had done them proud; the large table that could easily accommodate twelve was set with the finest silver and the best china and crystal.

The champagne flowed freely, and when Marie had laughingly asked what they were celebrating Uncle Jacques had responded, 'Why, my horse Supreme winning the Grand Prix de L'Arc de Triomphe, of course.'

'Such confidence,' Marie mocked. 'The race is not for another month yet.'

'I entirely agree with Jacques's sentiment,' Rayner inserted, and casting a sidelong glance at Marie, his grey eyes narrowing on her lovely face, he added, 'I never consider losing. What I want I go for.'

'And do you always get what you want?' Marie asked quietly, her golden eyes trapped by the intensity of his gaze.

'Yes,' he answered firmly, adding softly so only she could hear, 'As you are about to find out, my lovely.' And for a brief instant his large hand covered hers on the table in an intimate gesture.

Marie looked down at her plate, unnerved by his touch. He was flirting with her, and she was not sure how to deal with it. She lifted her fork with a hand that trembled, and picked at the food on her plate. Luckily no one appeared to have noticed the by-play between Rayner and herself, and the conversation flowed on around her. Sternly she told herself not to be so naïve. It was a chemical reaction to a handsome male, nothing more... And slowly she regained her calm poise.

Anna was a superb cook and the meal was excellent. They started with a seafood platter of oysters, langoustines and mussels, with a variety of dressings to choose from. The main course was beef Rossini with fresh *haricots verts* and tiny new potatoes. Then, in the French way, there was a variety of cheeses. For dessert there was home-made ice-cream, a magnificent chocolate and almond gâteau or fresh fruit salad.

The conversation was lively as the men started arguing over which was the best horse that had ever won the Arc. As the premier race of the French racing calendar, it was Jacques's lifetime ambition to train a horse to win it.

Marie chuckled over Aunt Celeste's opinion that the only reason they were leaving early in the morning to go and stay with a trainer friend and rival of Jacques was so Jacques could nobble his entry for the great race.

By the time they had finished eating and moved into the main salon for coffee, Marie felt quite relaxed. Rayner was a charming man and she had listened with growing pleasure to him all evening. It was obvious her grandpapa liked him, and Aunt Celeste became positively coy when he smiled at her.

After one such smile, Celeste teased, 'I am sure you must have some French blood in your veins; you have all the Gallic charm, and Rayner is a French name, surely.'

'I might possibly have a trace of French blood, but very much diluted. Mine is an Anglo-Saxon family registered in the Domesday Book, but I believe at the Norman invasion an ancestor of mine married a Norman chieftain's daughter—I suspect mainly to protect his lands. But as for my name, Rayner—it is pure Anglo-Saxon.'

Marie was intrigued by this insight into his family and, putting her coffee-cup down on the low table at the side of her chair, she was able to watch him as he sat at ease on the plush sofa, chatting to Celeste. He must have sensed her interest for his eyes lifted, alert and probing, trapping hers with a glittering intensity.

A shiver of apprehension trickled down her spine as he continued, 'Roughly translated, it means, "Warrior of Judgement".'

His voice was hard, and she had the odd premonition that his definition was aimed exclusively at her for some reason. Then he turned to Celeste and the moment was gone. Marie retrieved her coffee and took a welcome drink. She was becoming fanciful in her old age, she thought wryly.

She drained her coffee-cup and replaced it on the table, then settled back in the deep armchair, allowing the conversation to flow around her. It was arranged that Rayner

would spend the morning looking over the farm with
Henri, and Marie agreed to take him to Les Sables
d'Olonne in the afternoon. She was loath to admit it,
but the thought of spending time alone with him was
becoming more and more appealing.

Time and again her gaze was irresistibly drawn to him.
He was an intelligent and witty conversationalist, and
he fitted in with her family as if he had known them for
years. A few times he caught her eye and flashed her a
warm, intimate grin that made her pulse-rate rise
alarmingly.

Celeste and Jacques were the first to retire, with a kiss
for Henri and Marie, and a cordial goodnight to Rayner,
plus a promise to meet him the following weekend at
their stud farm.

Henri suggested to Rayner another brandy, and while
the two men shared a last drink Marie collected the
coffee-cups and returned them to the kitchen.

She returned to the salon, intending to say goodnight
and leave, when to her chagrin her grandpapa would not
hear of it, and with all the tact of a charging rhinoceros
he said, 'Rubbish, child, you have hardly said a word
all night. Rayner does not want to go to bed yet, it is
far too early for two youngsters like you. Speak to him
in his native language, make him feel at home.' And
with a brief kiss on her cheek he walked towards the
door. 'Don't forget to switch off the lights.' With
indecent haste, he left.

Marie's face burned with embarrassment, and hearing
Rayner laugh didn't help her composure one jot.

'Blunt man, your grandfather. The native language
bit was a gem,' he chuckled, and rising to his feet he
crossed the few paces separating them, to stop inches
away from her. 'But I like his ideas,' he opined throatily,

speaking in English for the first time since they were alone.

Blunt man, indeed—what Henri needed was a blunt instrument laid across his thick head, she thought furiously, and it took all her self-control to raise her head and face Rayner. 'I must apologise for my grandfather,' she said curtly, still furious with the old man. 'He does speak English, quite well in fact, but with the supreme arrogance of the truly French he refuses to do so.'

'Well, well... Your English upbringing can break through that cool mask of typically French *savoir-faire* you have portrayed so well all evening.' And catching her chin in the palm of his hand he tilted her head back.

She was unaware of the golden glitter in her topaz eyes—all she saw was the darkening gleam in Rayner's.

'I was beginning to wonder if I had imagined the temper that matched your red hair in the past,' he drawled mockingly.

His hand moved slightly lower to lightly grasp her throat. He was much too close for comfort, and she was humiliatingly conscious of the thundering beat of her heart, sure that he must hear it. 'I am not bad-tempered,' she denied curtly, and in an effort to put some space between them she stepped back. It didn't work as Rayner moved with her.

'No?' he queried cynically. His teeth flashed in a wicked grin as he brought his face threateningly close to hers. 'Or perhaps it is only with me that your passions rise.'

Black fire flared in the depths of his dark eyes, capable of burning her flesh, she thought fancifully, and, lowering her thick lashes to escape his penetrating gaze, she answered him with studied coolness.

'No. Grandpapa is irritating, that is all. Ever since his last heart attack he has had this idea he must marry me off,' she said flatly. 'I think he's worried that if anything happens to him I will be left on my own. I have told him it is stupid.' She tried a light laugh, but she wasn't sure she succeeded—even to her own ears it sounded more like a high-pitched squeak. 'I know he means well, but he insists on throwing me at every man of his acquaintance, so please just ignore him.'

'My dear Marie, are you sure that is the reason?' His hand tightened slightly on her throat, and she raised startled eyes to his. A shiver of fear coursed down her spine as she caught a brief glimpse of some undefinable emotion in their glittering depths. She blinked. She must have imagined it, she thought, as his eyes were again the cool grey of a cloudy day.

Rayner's hand fell from her throat and she breathed a sigh of relief, but it was short-lived, as his arms locked around her slender waist, bringing their lower bodies into close contact. She tensed, acutely sensitive to the feel of his hard muscular thighs pressed against her slender limbs.

'Of course I'm sure, what else could it be?' she said with all the confidence she could muster.

'It is quite simple, Marie. You are a very beautiful woman, and a great actress. You have that look of pure innocence that is very hard to fake. I take my hat off to you,' he said with cutting cynicism. 'I don't know how you do it, because I know to my cost that it is years since you were a virgin, and, once a girl has taste for it, she can't leave it alone.'

Marie cringed at his reference to the past, too shocked to speak—and what did he mean, to his cost? All he had suffered was a few hours' inconvenience, while she... She had taken years to get over the hurt, she thought bitterly.

'Henri is a very perceptive man, Marie. He might have been fooled by your look of purity in the beginning, but he knows as well as I do that eventually—how shall I put it?' He hesitated. 'Your lifestyle, will show on those beautiful features. Only today his housekeeper met us with a story of some beach orgy you had been to. I don't blame Henri for wanting to marry you off at the first opportunity. How old are you now? Twenty-five...?No. Sorry, I forgot for a moment, that was something else you lied about,' he grated contemptuously.

Marie listened, stunned by his scathing, sarcastic attack, and as the import of his words sunk in all semblance of her cool sophistication shot out of the window, to be replaced with mindless fury. How dared he judge her? She didn't give a damn if her house guest appeared tomorrow with a black eye, he deserved it. Her fingers curled into a fist between their two bodies.

But she never raised her hand. She did not know how it happened but suddenly she was pinned against the wall, her hands caught behind her back in one of Rayner's. With his other hand he again held her chin. She squirmed in his hold, but his fingers bit into the tender flesh of her neck, forcing her head back.

'Oh, no. No, Marie Doumerque, I won't tolerate violence from you ever again,' he hissed.

Her eyes stared into his for a second, naked with rage, then he lowered his head. His lips were harsh as they claimed hers.

Marie struggled, but the savage, bruising hunger of his kiss shocked her into immobility. His teeth bit sharply on her lower lip and she gasped. His tongue thrust deeply into her mouth. Wildly she wondered how a pleasant evening had deteriorated so rapidly, but as his hand slipped slowly from her throat to trail caressingly over her full breast and down to her slender waist, pulling her firmly against his hard frame, she stopped wondering...

His mouth gentled on hers, softly, seductively, wooing where before he had plundered. Heat surged through her body, she closed her eyes, and mindlessly gave herself up to the fires of passion he was igniting in her. Of their own volition, her hands stroked over his broad chest to grasp desperately at his wide shoulders, her legs turning weak as water.

She moaned deep in her throat when his lips left hers to press fervent kisses along her cheekbone, her eyelids, her brow, and once more her softly pouting mouth, while his hands roved the soft contours of her breasts, her buttocks, her stomach.

'Marie, you are as bewitchingly seductive as ever.' Rayner groaned the words against her mouth before leaning her back over his arm and trailing hot kisses down her throat to the shadowed valley of her full breasts.

But when his long fingers eased under the neckline and cupped her breast, his thumb lightly grazing the already hard nipple, she murmured, 'No.' The word was more a sigh than an objection.

'Yes. I want you, and I know you want me, but not here, let's go upstairs,' Rayner prompted harshly.

At his words, Marie shuddered back to reality. God, what was she doing? Her hands slid from around Rayner's neck to push frantically at his muscular chest. She caught him by surprise, and she was free. Scarlet with embarrassment, she straightened her dress with hands that shook. Rayner reached for her, but she darted across the room as if all the hounds in hell were after her.

Had she learnt nothing in all these years? she berated herself. How could she have fallen into his arms again, just like a stupid teenager? She turned to face him, but making sure to keep a good distance between them. She would not run away in her own home.

'I take it that means no,' Rayner chuckled.

She was furious; her hair had long since fallen from its chignon, and she knew she must look a sight. His early insulting summation of her morals echoed in her brain, and what irked her most was that, while her traitorous body still trembled and ached for his love-making, he had completely regained his composure and was actually laughing at her—just as he had the first time. A sense of *déjà vu* overwhelmed her. Her fury withered and died.

She squared her shoulders; she had struggled for years to regain her pride, her self-respect, and she could not allow him to believe he could intimidate her. Rayner moved towards her, still smiling, and she stretched out her arm, her hand up in a regal gesture.

'I find nothing amusing in this situation, Monsieur Millard. As you are a guest in this house I will not tell you what I really think of you. Suffice it to say I find your opinions and behaviour insulting in the extreme. You will understand our arrangements for tomorrow are now cancelled. I'm sure you are more than capable of going sightseeing on your own, and if you are any kind of gentleman, which I seriously doubt, you will make your stay here as short as possible.' Marie did not wait for his response, and turning on her heel she walked towards the door, flinging over her shoulder, 'The sooner you go to your room, the sooner I can close down the house for the night.' She flung open the door, and turned with one hand on the light switch and the other on her hip. 'After you, sir,' she prompted sarcastically.

Rayner stared at her silently for several seconds, then with a slight nod of his head he strode purposefully towards the door, his expression unreadable.

Marie inwardly sighed with relief—thank God, he was going to do as she said. Her self-control was stretched to its limit, and she doubted if she could hold her poise much longer.

But as he came abreast of her he stopped, towering over her. Marie flashed a wary glance up at his handsome face. Now what?

'I am sorry if I offended you, Marie. It was never my intention.'

'It's all right,' she said stiffly, just wanting him to leave.

'Believe me, Marie, I was only teasing.' Rayner looked deep into the soft topaz eyes that were bravely trying to subdue him, and his lips curved in a rueful smile. 'I guess you have changed more than I thought. You used to be able to take a joke,' he drawled softly.

'A joke.' Marie felt herself weakening. He looked woefully contrite—had she misunderstood the situation? No, she could not be that wrong.

'Yes, a joke—perhaps not in the best of taste. But surely you can understand? I have watched you all night, so cool, serene, the perfect lady, and I just had to find out if there was anything left of the young Goldie I once knew.' He hesitated and, stretching out one long finger, he gently stroked down her soft cheek. 'And loved,' he husked throatily. 'I meant what I told you earlier. I have thought a lot about you over the years. What man can forget his first love?' he mused. His grey eyes, soft and shining, smiled into hers, throwing her thoughts into chaos once again. 'I did not mean the things I said to you, I only said them to get under your skin, break through your icy reserve, to discover if the passionate girl of my memories still existed.'

Marie blushed bright red. She could not deny he aroused a wanton passion in her she had not known she possessed. But his assertion that he had loved her was the main reason for the surge of heat turning her cheeks red. She stood mute, a wild tumble of conflicting thoughts spinning in her head. Dared she believe him? Had she completely misread him before? And now, tonight... She didn't know what to think.

'I'm sorry, I have embarrassed you yet again. Look, I promise to behave as a model of decorum, if you will consent to be my guide for the next few days. I will go to bed now. On my own,' he quipped. 'Like a good little boy.'

She was grateful for all the years that had bred in her self-restraint. If she went with her instincts she would have flung herself joyfully into his arms. Instead she scrutinised his handsome features, looking for any sign of deceit. There was none... His firm lips curved in a grin that was penitent, and somehow pleading. Marie felt her own lips curve in response. He looked like a young boy caught with his hand in the cookie jar, she thought tenderly.

'Please, I won't sleep until I know I am forgiven, and you will be my guide,' Rayner prompted in a voice laced with laughter.

'Yes, of course.' She had made her decision—she would take him at face value, and hope she had not got her signals crossed...

CHAPTER THREE

MARIE woke to the sound of a car door slamming, and for a moment she was confused. The pale light of dawn barely brushed the sky with a rosy haze. Who could be arriving? Then the memory of the previous day's events surfaced and, jumping out of bed, she dashed to the window in time to see the tail-lights of Uncle Jacques's car disappear down the drive.

She yawned and stretched like a lazy cat, her sleep-softened features glowing with a self-indulgent smile, as she scurried back to her bed and crawled under the covers. It was far too early to get up, and there would be no one about for at least another couple of hours.

She had fallen into bed last night and gone out like a light, much to her surprise, but now she found it impossible to recapture that oblivious state. Instead her mind insisted on replaying every minute, every word spoken, since her incredible meeting with Rayner again. A host of conflicting emotions tumbled around in her head. Her body flushed with heat at the memory of Rayner's passionate embrace and her own willing response.

She squirmed restlessly on the bed. The defensive cocoon she had painstakingly woven around the sensual side of her nature had crumbled to dust at one touch from Rayner. She was as fatally attracted to him now as she had been years ago, and the thought terrified her. When he had laughed last night at her easy capitulation, she had been forcibly reminded of the other time he had laughed after loving her...

In her mind's eye she saw his gloriously naked body, silvered by moonlight, relaxed and satiated, lying beside her. She shivered as she recalled the rest.

He had laughed out loud. 'A hippy! Wait till I tell my father.'

With one sentence, one word—'hippy'—he had destroyed her youthful dream of love. The truth had been like a knife in her heart. She meant nothing to him. In his eyes she was the lowest of the low. Someone to fool around with and laugh over with his father.

Deaf and blind to anything but her own hurt, she had leapt to her feet, struggling with her clothes, and crying hysterically. Rayner had tried to stop her, and she had fought him like a wild thing, and that was how the police had found them...

Flinging off the covers, she jumped out of bed—she did not want to think of the rest, it was too painful. Raising her hands to her head, she brushed her hair off her face. It needed washing. Perhaps if she concentrated on mundane pursuits, she told herself sternly, she might get a respite from her fluctuating emotions.

Rayner had said last night she was his first love. If that was true, and she had been wrong, it still did not change anything. Seven years ago he had been miles above her, financially, socially, in every way there was. She had recognised that long ago and accepted it.

She stripped off her flimsy nightgown and walked into the bathroom. Turning on the shower, she picked up a bottle of shampoo and stepped beneath the soothing spray. Vigorously she washed her hair, then, turning her face up, she let the water rinse through the long tresses. Next she gently soaped herself all over, her hands lingering sensuously on her full breasts. Rayner had touched her there...

With a snort of self-disgust, she turned the cold water on full blast. Finally she stepped out of the shower and, roughly wrapping a large bath-sheet around her shivering body, she marched into the bedroom. She stopped in mid-stride, as an intriguing thought popped into her head.

Rayner was no longer above her in every way. She was a successful career woman of good breeding and family. Even her father, Tom—mainly because he was dead, she acknowledged cynically—was respectable now. His paintings were much sought-after and commanded exorbitant prices.

Yes, she mused, as she briskly towelled herself dry and quickly slipped on clean underwear, something had changed. Now she could meet Rayner on an equal basis. Feeling oddly exhilarated she sat down at the dressing-table, and switching on her hair-drier she began to dry her hair. Maybe, just maybe, she thought wistfully, the next few days with Rayner could be the start of something good...

Marie eyed the gleaming silver monster with some resentment, before sliding reluctantly into the passenger seat.

'I can't see why we couldn't use my car. It's much easier to park,' she stated bluntly. Since sharing a light lunch with her grandpapa and Rayner, she felt as if she had been run over by a steamroller. She had been ordered to take her swimming gear, told they were dining out, and finally that Rayner was driving, and they were using his car. 'He didn't need a guide, he only wanted a willing slave,' she muttered resentfully under her breath.

'Fasten your seatbelt, and stop muttering,' Rayner drawled as he slid into the driving-seat and, with an economy of movement, started the engine and drove off.

She flushed at his rebuke and, casting him a sidelong glance, she was struck once again by the hard, chiselled perfection of his profile, her eyes lowered to where his hands rested lightly on the steering-wheel. His fingers were long, the nails short and neatly clipped... Her breasts tingled and she could almost feel the touch of his hands on her body.

'Turn right,' she said curtly, as she hastily looked out of the window. She closed her eyes for an instant, dizzy with fear, for herself and what this man could do to her.

'I know. There's no need to give me directions. Henri has already done that,' Rayner responded drily.

'Then what do you need me for?' she shot back.

He flashed her a devilish grin. 'Need you ask, Marie?' he drawled suggestively, then with a chuckle he added, 'Relax. We are two people on holiday. The sun is shining, it is a beautiful day, and you and I are going to have fun. According to your grandfather you spend far too long locked up in your ivory tower poring over your books.'

Marie sighed. 'Trust him,' she said ruefully. There was some truth in her grandpapa's words. She had spent all morning working on her fourth children's story. So why not relax? Slowly she felt the tension drain out of her, as she settled back against the rich leather upholstery. She smoothed the cream cotton of the classic shirt-waister dress down over her thighs, and stretched her long legs out in front of her. She could not resist one dig at Rayner as he took a corner rather wide.

'Don't forget, we drive on the right in France.'

His lips quirked in amusement, but he made no comment.

Marie sat silently surveying the passing scenery for the time it took to reach the outskirts of the seaside town of Les Sables d'Olonne, but the silence was companionable.

'Right—straight to the beach, this heat is killing me,' he complained, mopping his brow with one large hand in an exaggerated gesture.

Marie chuckled and, getting out of the car, swung her tote bag over her shoulder. 'Straight to the beach,' she parroted.

He clasped her slender hand in his and quipped, 'Lead on, Macduff. No—it should be MacDoumerque.'

'That was terrible,' she groaned, but laughed anyway.

Hand in hand they walked around the long length of the harbour. On the far side were the large warehouses and freezer houses of the co-operative fishing industry. A stretch of dull water separated them from the main roadway where all the buildings were old and mostly housed small shops, bars and a good smattering of excellent fish restaurants. They crossed the old town square and turned the corner.

Marie was hardly aware of where they were walking. In a dream-like state, she pointed out the newish casino, and the wide sweep of the mile-long beach, with its elegant promenade of old and new buildings cleverly intermingled.

Rayner negotiated the hiring of a beach cabin, and putting an arm around her shoulders he led her down to the golden sand. Stopping at the door of the cabin, he nuzzled her neck, murmuring, 'We can easily share, hmm?'

She flushed scarlet—the idea of disrobing in front of Rayner set off a million different images in her mind, all of them censored.

'No way. I'll go first,' she responded bluntly, wondering what on earth was happening to her. His laughter rung in her ears as she closed the door behind her.

A few minutes later she nervously opened the door and, taking a deep breath, stepped out. It was stupid to feel shy, but she did. Plenty of women bathed topless on this beach and her green bikini was quite conservative by most standards. She had worn it dozens of times and never felt embarrassed, but when Rayner turned to look at her she had to fight down an urge to fold her arms over her chest.

His eyes swept in deliberate appraisal over her, lingering on the full curve of her breasts, the long line of her thighs, and back to her face. Dark colour flushed over his hard features, and he made no effort to hide his masculine appreciation.

'You are stunning, absolutely beautiful. My God! You certainly have grown up,' he opined raspingly.

Marie turned scarlet under his searching gaze, and did fold her arms in a protective gesture.

'You can't be shy, surely. Not at your age,' he drawled mockingly, and with a laugh he brushed past her into the cabin.

Marie shook her head wryly, acknowledging that Rayner was far too sophisticated for her... She had never taken a man to bed or even dated properly since Rayner. She was a bad case of arrested development, had been for seven years, that was for sure...

The truth of her thoughts was clearly demonstrated in the next minute when he walked out of the cabin. Her topaz eyes widened in wonder at the perfection of his male form. She couldn't look away. Hungrily she measured the width of his shoulders, his broad chest lightly dusted with dark golden hairs. Her eyes followed the trail of body hair down past his navel to where it

disappeared beneath brief black trunks. She gulped at
his blatant masculine strength, his long legs, lithe and
strong. His skin gleamed like polished gold satin, and
she had an incredible urge to reach out and touch him.
She actually raised her hand.

'Well, have you seen enough? Will I do?' Rayner
queried, amusement evident in his tone.

She winced at his words. She was behaving like a star-
struck teenager, and, dropping her hand, she tried to
redress the balance by cheekily tilting her head to one
side, and studying him through half-closed eyes. 'I think
so, but ask me after,' she drawled in what she hoped
was a sexy voice, and turning on her heel she ran towards
the sea.

Marie dived headlong into the crashing breakers of
the Atlantic Ocean, welcoming the cool water on her
overheated flesh. She was an excellent swimmer, and
setting off in a steady crawl she was soon some fifty
yards from the beach. She trod water for a moment and
turned to look back for Rayner, when something grabbed
her ankle. In a second she was under the water, arms
like steel traps pinning her to a hard male body. She did
not need to look any further. Rayner, his features dis-
torted by the water, loomed over her, his mouth crushed
down on hers and she was powerless to do anything about
it—she didn't want to...

They surfaced locked in each other's arms. Marie took
a great gulp of air as Rayner finally broke the kiss.
Somehow her slender arms were wrapped around his
neck, her long legs intimately entwined with his strong
ones. A moan escaped her, as the moist heat of his mouth
moved slowly down to her cleavage. She was aware of
nothing except the fierce need he aroused in her.

His teeth bit gently over a pert nipple clearly outlined
through the fine damp fabric of her bikini, then his

mouth claimed it completely. She forgot everything, where they were, the people around them.

The raw sound of the surf pounding matched the pounding of her heart. Her lips found his sun-bronzed shoulder, her teeth grazed his satin flesh, her hand flattened on his back, tracing the muscle and sinew—it was only when they submerged again that she was jolted back to her senses. She forgot to breathe and swallowed a good deal of the Atlantic in the process...

Spluttering and coughing, she felt a complete idiot, while Rayner held her lightly under the arms, supporting her in the water, and laughing at her distress.

'Well, have you reached a verdict?' he asked, his silver gaze lowering to her breasts. 'Or shall I draw my own conclusions?' he drawled mockingly.

'What?' she gasped stupidly. She was suddenly aware that her hard nipples proudly proclaimed her aroused state.

'You said you would tell me later if I would do. So... this is later, and I want an answer.'

Marie bravely looked straight at him, her topaz eyes wide and honest. She could not read his expression— with the sun behind him his face was shadowed—but she told him the truth. 'You would more than do for any woman.' Her full lips curved in an enchanting smile. 'But I think you already know that, and you don't need compliments from me. I'm sure you're conceited enough already,' she opined cheekily.

Rayner made a grab for her, but she was ready for him. They spent the next couple of hours frolicking like children in the water, finally returning to the beach and collapsing breathless on to the huge beach towel.

Marie was amazed at the easy friendship that had developed between them. She was very conscious of his superb sun-kissed body next to hers, but somehow the tension had gone.

Later, dressed once again, they strolled hand in hand around the cluster of little streets behind the promenade, and finally, as darkness fell, down to the old harbour.

They dined on huge platters of seafood in a cosy little restaurant, and talked. By the time the bottle of wine Rayner had ordered was empty, they had covered art, the theatre and music, and found they shared compatible views on most of them. It was when Marie had tried to explain the intricacies of French politics, and the escapades of Madame Le Pen in her efforts to stop her estranged husband getting elected, that they had collapsed into laughter.

Rayner flatly refused to believe it and they were still arguing for and against the woman's view when they returned to the château. It had been a perfect day and set the tone for the rest of the week.

Marie eyed the contents of her wardrobe balefully. It was the last day of Rayner's stay—tomorrow; on Friday, he was leaving for Jacques's stud farm, and the following day returning to England. Today was her last chance to impress him, and she wanted to wear something that would knock his socks off... Unfortunately all her clothes tended to be conservative: Chanel suits, classic-styled dresses and matching country casuals.

She sighed. Who was she kidding? She just wasn't the sexy type. In that she was completely wrong—her model-girl looks, her full, high breasts and narrow waist, the gentle flare of her hips, coupled with a loose-limbed, gliding walk, were a sensuous invitation to any man, but she was completely unaware of it.

She had lain awake for most of the night, hot, aching with a hunger to feel once again the passion of Rayner's lovemaking, and in the cool light of dawn she had finally admitted to herself that she loved him, and probably always had, and always would...

Over the last few days they had gone everywhere together; he had been a perfect companion, but to her chagrin he had made no attempt to further their relationship. He had behaved with model decorum, more like a brother than a lover. He had touched her frequently, an arm around her shoulder, a helping hand at her elbow, a brief hug, or, in the car, when he wanted to draw attention to something, a strong tanned hand on her thigh.

Marie groaned, her flesh tingling ecstatically as she remembered the touch of his fingers against her skin. It was ironic, but for ages she had thought she was cold, frigid, because of Rayner. Now she knew the reverse was true. This torrent of emotion, and need, the fierce hunger that made her want to abandon all pride and actually try to seduce him, completely overwhelmed her cautious nature. She almost laughed out loud. She didn't care. She wanted him...

Finally she decided on the buttercup silk, the dress she had worn on the first night of his stay. It was a daring choice—the prim, neatly buttoned front fastened high on her breast-bone, and tied with a halter, but left half her back bare. She surveyed her reflection in the mirror, and with a small secretive smile she unfastened the top three buttons, exposing a goodly amount of cleavage. Perhaps Rayner would remember unfastening the very same buttons. At least, she hoped he would.

Her plan was working, Marie decided, a tiny smile twitching her lips, as she settled in the passenger seat of the Jaguar and deftly fastened the seatbelt.

Her smile grew even wider when Rayner got in the car and turned towards her, his hands reaching out to her, and her heart raced with anticipation of his touch. Her golden eyes reflected all her love and adoration as they lifted to his. She stared up into cold grey eyes, icy with anger, and froze.

'I despise women who openly display their very obvious charms, and so long as you are in my company I will not allow you to behave like a tramp.' His long fingers deftly buttoned the front of her dress and she was too humiliated to stop him. 'Do I make myself clear?' he demanded harshly.

Marie flinched at the scathing contempt in his tone, and unable to meet his gaze she bent her head, and mumbled a feeble excuse. 'Yes, but I was hot.'

They drove for almost half an hour in silence. Marie could feel the tension building in the close confines of the car, and she searched desperately for something to say. Her nerves were at breaking-point. She wanted to scream her innocence, tell him she was not that sort of girl, but she could not bring herself to dispense with her hard-won sophisticated image so easily.

It was her own stupid fault; she was no vamp. She recognised, too late, that to a mature predatory male like Rayner her blatant attempt to seduce him must have seemed disgusting. She groaned inwardly. Not an auspicious start to their last day together, but she needn't have worried, because in the next second he pulled the car into the side of the road and stopped.

'What——?' was as far as she got before Rayner, unfastening his seatbelt, bent over her. His mouth took relentless possession of hers, parting her lips in a long passionate kiss.

'I'm sorry for shouting at you before—please forgive me,' he whispered against her mouth. 'But I want you so badly, Marie,' he groaned. 'You can't know what it has cost me to keep my hands off you the last few days.'

And his hands stroked urgently over her quivering, overheated body. She could feel the thudding of his heart beneath her hand, and she heard the breath catch in his throat as, with a terrific effort of self-control, he eased away from her.

Taking a few deep breaths, he sat back in his seat. 'I think we'd better drive on before I disgrace myself completely in your eyes,' he stated hardly.

Marie stared at him through passion-hazed eyes, noting the dark flush on his handsome face and the self-derogatory smile that curved the corner of his mouth.

'You could never do that, Rayner,' she said breathlessly. In the clear morning sunlight she could see the tiny lines fanning out from his eyes, the beloved mouth, soft and oh, so sensuous, the harsh scar... She lifted a slender hand and lovingly traced the line of his wound. He stiffened, tension in every line of his body.

'Does that bother you?' he demanded harshly.

'No, no, Rayner, how could you think that?' she quickly reassured him, touched by the flash of vulnerability she had seen in his eyes. 'I would love you whatever...' she murmured. She had not meant to admit her feelings but the words had just slipped out.

He flashed her a brief, startled glance, and a gleam of pure masculine triumph lit his eyes. 'Ah, Marie, you are delightful.' And, giving her a broad smile, he added, 'This is going to be the best day yet.'

It was a glorious afternoon. La Rochelle lay like a perfect jewel in the hot sun. It was an ancient town steeped in history, the medieval buildings leaning over the tiny narrow streets that led to the small inner harbour. The entrance to the sea was only a few yards wide, and guarded by massive stone towers and the ancient city wall.

A few yachts lay at anchor, their pennants fluttering lightly in the breeze, and the restaurants and bars that surrounded the harbour were busy with the lunchtime crowd. A smattering of tourists took pictures of the ancient fortifications, while the more sophisticated residents lingered over their coffee and brandy.

Rayner held her hand and together they roamed the narrow streets. They stopped at a small restaurant on the harbour, and ate fresh crab salad and shared a half-carafe of wine, because of the driving.

Marie had never seen Rayner so relaxed before—it was as if he had shed ten years and was once more a carefree young man. They laughed, talked and teased, and occasionally their eyes would meet and cling, sending a deeper, more intimate message. She wished she could bottle the day, and keep it forever.

Later they wandered down to the tower guarding the harbour and Rayner spanned her waist with strong hands and lifted her up on to the ancient wall. They walked along for a few hundred yards to where La Lanterne, another tower, rose majestically up to the sky. It was open to the public and Marie said impulsively,

'I want to stand on top of the world today, Rayner. Please can we go up?'

'Yes, of course, my love. Today is yours, and if you want to walk up a few hundred stairs I will force my old legs to carry me,' he teased.

She cast a glance at the legs in question as he walked with the easy, natural stride of a confident man up the few steps to the entrance kiosk inside the old stone building, and her heart beat a little faster. His pale grey trousers clung lovingly to his firm buttocks and tightly sinewed thighs, and she fought back a sharp erotic flush of longing. He turned and their eyes met; Rayner smiled, a knowing look in his grey eyes.

He had read her mind again. She laughed out loud, and almost tripped over her feet in her haste to reach him.

It was dark inside the circular room, the only light the natural light that shone through the oblong slits in the wall that served as windows. A narrow spiral staircase lead to the floors above. Marie stopped to read with interest the detailed history of the place as described on documents displayed in large glass cases attached to the wall.

It had been a prison. For centuries convicts from all over France had been imprisoned there while waiting to be shipped to the infamous Devil's Island, even into the twentieth century. She followed Rayner up to the next level and another large, circular room.

The place was unbelievable. Cut into the solid stone walls were the names and dates of some of the inmates; an intricate carving of a sailing ship caught her eye, a work of years, and, carved in the wood of the floor, a draught-board. She had a vivid mental image of sailors in old-fashioned dress, squatting on the floor to play chess. Eagerly she turned to Rayner.

'Isn't this fabulous?' she cried, bubbling with enthusiasm.

'I doubt the poor bastards who stayed here would have shared your view,' Rayner responded curtly.

A frown creased her smooth brow—he sounded quite angry, she thought, but before she could wonder at it her eyes were caught by an inscription cut into the wall beside one of the turret windows.

'Rayner, Rayner, come and see this—what a coincidence, this man was from Whitby. ''Richard Douglas of Whitby taken in the Triumph of New York 19 January 1782.'''

A lump formed in her throat as she read it out loud. She looked around expecting to see Rayner, and instead caught a glimpse of his oddly tense back as he disappeared up the stairs to the next level.

Her earlier enthusiasm for the ancient building vanished. She stared around with sightless eyes, and the sombre atmosphere of the place enveloped her. She imagined all the thousands of men who must have stayed in this place awaiting transportation to the dreaded island, or maybe even death. She shivered, not with cold, but with the echoing cries of a thousand lost souls that rang in her head.

Marie shook her head to dispel the images of the past, and shrugging her shoulders she hurried on up the staircase. She found Rayner at a higher level where the room was totally different. Big, rectangular windows opened out on to a small walkway circling the building, and Rayner was outside leaning over the balustrade staring out over the sea.

She hesitated for a moment before joining him, struck by the dark brooding look on his handsome face. What was wrong? she asked herself; he had hardly spoken a word to her since entering the building.

Hearing her approach, he swung round—for a sickening moment she thought he looked contemptuous, but it must have been a trick of the light because when she reached him he was smiling.

'Rayner, why the hurry?' she asked in a determinedly cheerful voice, and standing next to him she slid her arm through his. 'You should read the inscriptions, they're great.'

'Hell, but you are an insensitive bitch.' He glared at her, his grey eyes chips of ice in the sharp contours of his face. 'I did read the inscription, but I doubt if the poor sod who engraved it shared your enthusiasm for his prison,' he drawled with mocking cynicism.

'I know that,' she said softly, shocked and hurt by his venomous comment. 'But——'

He did not give her a chance to explain. 'Come on and I'll show you one I found.' And leading her up to the next level he pointed to another inscription and read out loud, ' "Sacred to the memory of William Friethy, gunner of the *Lively* Privateer. 15 October 1778. Unfortunately shot dead trying to escape." ' His cold eyes raked her from head to foot, and his sensuous lips curled in a contemptuous sneer, as he added, 'Now, isn't that fun?'

'I didn't mean it was fun, only that this prison is interesting,' she tried to defend herself, dismayed by his change in attitude. She could not understand what had come over him.

'Interesting,' he grated. 'Tell me, Goldie darling, did you find the night you and I went to jail interesting?' His fingers bit into the soft flesh of her arm, and she winced with the pain. 'Do you imagine for one single second I enjoyed being in prison?' he snarled, his grey eyes black with rage as he took her roughly by the arm.

'Please, Rayner, you're hurting me,' she said in a tight voice, his remarks about the past filling her with an inexplicable fear. After all, one night in an English country jail could hardly be compared to staying in this place, she thought confusedly, and did not realise she had spoken her thoughts out loud.

He dropped her arm as though she had leprosy. 'One night?' A dark brow rose sardonically. 'Who are you trying to fool, Marie?'

'I am——'

'What the hell, let's get out of here, I can't stand the place.'

Marie did not argue; she was too confused, and she regretted whatever it was that had spoiled their perfect day.

Rayner hustled her outside and to the car. He did not give her a chance to question him, but once in the car he pulled her into his arms and kissed her with a fierce savage hunger that had her senses reeling in seconds. Finally he broke the kiss and drew back to look down on her, his grey eyes darkened as they met her bewildered golden ones.

'Ah, Marie, I've wanted to do that for hours. I need you in my arms, in my bed. I want you so badly. Forgive me for being such a boor at the tower, but I can't seem to handle my sexual frustration around you.'

She listened to his explanation in a daze of happiness. 'It's the same for me, Rayner,' she said softly, all her love and longing reflected in her topaz eyes.

'I wanted to do this with champagne and roses, but I can wait no longer, the suspense is killing me.' His voice was suddenly thick with tension. 'I'm trying to ask you to marry me, Marie. Please say yes.'

Her eyes widened in shock, then flinging her arms around his neck she scattered kisses all over his face. 'Oh, yes, Rayner, yes.' She could not believe her luck, all her wildest dreams had come true. 'Are you sure you want to marry me?' she had to ask, still hardly daring to believe it.

'You are the only woman I could marry, Marie. That is, if you don't strangle me before I get the chance,' he teased, and catching her wrists he folded them gently on his chest, then folded her in his arms. 'Behave, woman, we have a lot to discuss, and I must leave tomorrow. I thought Thursday, three weeks from today, in your parish church.'

'Yes, Rayner.'

'We won't be able to have much of a honeymoon—I've had too much time off already. So if you will settle for a couple of days in Paris and then back to England? Later we can have a proper honeymoon.'

'Yes, Rayner.'

'Are you always going to be this agreeable?' he asked, laughing.

'Yes, Rayner.' Lying in his arms, confident of his love, she would have agreed to anything...

When they finally returned to the château, her grandpapa was delighted but not surprised at the news, as Rayner had formally asked his permission the evening before. Marie was astonished, but secretly pleased. In her besotted state, to her eyes it confirmed that at last she had Rayner's respect as well as love.

CHAPTER FOUR

THE wedding veil was old and very fragile, the lace as delicate as a spider's web; it had belonged to Marie's great-grandmother, as had the dress she wore. She put it on with hands that trembled. It fell over her thick Titian hair in gentle folds, held in place by a tiara of cleverly woven fresh flowers.

She stared at the reflection in the mirror, and her topaz eyes looked back at her, luminous with wonder and joy. She knew she had never looked more beautiful, or ever would again. It was her wedding-day and she was ecstatically happy.

Rayner was her ideal man, and so supportive. He had called her every night for the past three weeks and they had talked for hours. He had quickly allayed her slight fears about her work, when quite out of the blue Alain, her publisher, had informed her that her children's books had been sold to television, for a children's series, and they would like her to advise on the graphics. Rayner had given his whole-hearted approval.

'Marie, it's time to leave for the church.' Celeste's voice jolted her back to the present. She stood up, and, smoothing the soft ivory satin of her wedding gown over her slim hips, she walked downstairs.

Marie smiled in delight as young Janine, dressed in swirling pink taffeta and looking very grown-up, left the house with her mother. Then minutes later it was Marie's turn.

Every seat was taken in the small church—the whole village had turned out. Marie was filled with the pride of every Doumerque woman who had taken their vows in this church for generations. She straightened her shoulders, her gaze fixed on the tall silver-haired man who stood with his back to her at the altar. She moved down the aisle on her grandpapa's arm, with a confident step, to join the man she loved...

She wasn't aware of the service, her whole being centred on the man by her side, his strong hand firmly clasping hers. She could not take her eyes from Rayner's face. His grey eyes burnt into hers glittering with a fierce emotion. She heard his voice deep and steady say, 'I will,' and her own response was a soft whisper in comparison. Rayner lowered his head, and she raised her face to him. His lips, cool and firm, brushed hers very lightly. Then as though compelled he gathered her in his arms, his mouth seeking hers in a kiss of fierce possession.

Marie floated through the reception at the château in a golden glow of happiness. The popular opinion, as she finally slid into the front seat of the gleaming silver Jaguar, was that a more radiant bride had never graced *Le Petit Château*.

'It was the most perfect wedding ever,' Marie declared, and with a deep sigh of pure contentment she settled back against the soft leather upholstery. She turned her head slightly, the better to study the handsome profile of her new husband. 'Don't you agree, Rayner?' she prompted teasingly.

'I am not an expert on the subject, but as weddings go I would say ours took the cake,' Rayner responded, tongue in cheek.

Marie groaned out loud. 'That is a terrible pun, Rayner, but I love you anyway,' she laughingly replied.

His fair head turned towards her, studying her intently for a long moment, his silvery gaze oddly enigmatic.

Then he turned his attention back to the road. 'I wonder,' he murmured.

'What did you say?' she asked, not sure she had heard him properly.

'I wondered if I had told you how beautiful you looked in your wedding gown,' he drawled, and with a brief sideways glance he added, 'And that green thing is lovely as well.'

She chuckled. 'I doubt Chanel would appreciate your description—"that green thing",' she mocked.

'So what do I know about ladies' clothes?' he quipped.

A lot more than he was admitting to, Marie thought ruefully, her gaze resting lightly on his muscular frame. The expertly tailored pearl-grey suit he wore lent him a sophisticated elegance that could not hide the raw animal magnetism of the man. He knew all about women, she was not fool enough to believe otherwise, but a self-satisfied smile curved her lips as she hugged the thought to herself. Now he was all hers...

'Why don't you try to get some sleep? It's about a three-hour drive to Paris, and I don't want you to fall asleep on me later, hmm?'

Marie tingled all over at the thought of the night ahead; she was longing to belong to Rayner completely, but she still could not stop a blush rising to her cheek-bones at the sensuous implication of his words. She slithered down in her seat and, casting a sidelong glance at Rayner, she said cheekily, 'Yes, o, master,' and closed her eyes.

Marie stood in the middle of the ornate marble and gold bathroom, a worried frown marring her smooth brow. They had arrived at the George V Hotel some hours pre-viously, and somehow nothing had gone as she had imagined. Rayner seemed withdrawn, solemn, and she did not know what to do about it.

Their suite was perfect, the sitting-room comfortable but elegant, decorated in old rose and gold, the furniture tasteful antiques. They had dined in the room, but the conversation had been stilted. Rayner had made some phone calls, then calmly told her he had a business meeting the following afternoon, but he was sure she could amuse herself for half a day. Marie had been unable to hide her disappointment, and Rayner had laughed.

'Don't worry. I'll leave you too tired to do anything, you'll be glad of the rest.'

'Confident macho man,' she'd quipped, trying to smile, but she could not help thinking it was not very romantic.

The bedroom, on the other hand, was. A symphony in white, all thick-pile carpet and floating drapes, but Rayner's comment when he saw it had upset her even more.

'All white, rather sterile. Hardly conducive to an interesting sex life, is it, Goldie?' he had queried mockingly, and with a careless gesture he'd reached out and trailed his hand from her throat over her breast to her waist, then pulled her towards him. She had stiffened in shock and pleasure at his touch. She'd wanted to object to his use of her old name, but never got the chance as he'd continued, 'Still, I'm sure it won't inhibit you.' His lips had brushed hers, and her lips had parted of their own volition. Rayner had not taken up the invitation she offered. 'My sensuous little wife,' he'd mocked softly, and spinning her around he'd patted her bottom. 'You use the bathroom first.'

It was stupid, but true. She was hiding in the bathroom. She had showered and donned the exquisite white négligé fifteen minutes ago, but had not the nerve to walk into the bedroom. Taking a deep breath, Marie straightened her shoulders; one last look in the mirror told her she had nothing to be ashamed of—the trouble was, she thought nervously most of it was on show. The négligé was virtually diaphanous...

Marie, my girl, you are a married woman, not an innocent teenager, she lectured herself sternly. Rayner would expect a woman in his bed and she was not going to disappoint him, she vowed, and with a defiant toss of her head she walked out of the bathroom.

'Your turn, Rayner.' She managed to speak normally, but her heart raced at the sight of him. He had already discarded all of his clothes except for his briefs. He was a superb male animal, dangerously so.

Bravely she faced him. He made no move, but the very air of the room seemed charged with an electric current of sensualism. Rayner's dark silver eyes seemed to pierce her soul. Proudly she stood as he studied her near naked form, his gaze lingering on the hard outline of her nipples against the flimsy fabric, and lower to the soft curve of her hips and thighs. She exulted in his scrutiny, her own gaze sweeping over his broad shoulders, the mat of soft hair on his muscular chest. She noted his harsh intake of breath, the sudden rise and fall of his chest, and when her glance slid lower she gasped at his obvious arousal.

'I hope you don't mind, but I'm going to have to skip the shower,' he growled, and in one lithe movement he had covered the space separating them, his hands quickly divested her of her robe and the delicate spaghetti straps of her nightgown were pushed slowly down her arms.

'I don't mind at all,' she said huskily. The fact that looking at her could arouse him instantly thrilled her and gave her confidence.

Boldly she wrapped her slender arms around his waist, and nuzzled the soft hair of his chest. His masculine scent, the hard heat of his muscular body, fascinated her. All her inhibitions vanished with the feel of his satin-smooth skin beneath her fingers. She tilted her head back and slid her hands up his broad back, tracing the muscle and sinew with tactile delight. Their eyes met, and her face flushed with hectic colour at the smouldering desire she saw in the darkening depths of his.

Rayner lowered his head, his lips brushed hers and she savoured the sweetness, while wanting more. He teased her mouth with licking, biting kisses until her lips moistly parted, and she was engulfed in wonderful erotic sensations, the fulfilment of all her dreams.

'What do you want, Marie?' he groaned hoarsely. 'Tell me, I have to hear you say it.' His strong hands forced her arms down and in a second he slipped her gown from her trembling body. 'Say it,' he demanded harshly, his palms cupping her breasts, his thumbs gently grazing the rigid peaks.

'I want you to make love to me,' she told him honestly, achingly. Her body was on fire for his. She brought her fingers to lock in the silky thickness of his silver hair, moulding her body to his. Somewhere in the back of her mind she was amazed at her own brazenness, but she did not care. She wanted him with an urgency that long years of deprivation had created.

'Oh, Marie,' he rasped as he kissed her, his tongue probing, pleasuring and then ravishing. He swept her up in his arms and in a few short strides placed her gently on the king-size bed, instantly joining her.

Leaning on one elbow, he bent over her, and with one tanned hand traced the outline of her quivering body, over the peak of her breast, the indentation of her waist, the flare of her hips and thighs down to her ankles, and slowly, oh, so slowly, back. His hand lingered at the apex of her thighs, and she groaned aloud her need.

'Exquisite,' he rasped.

'So are you,' she moaned. Her own small hand lovingly traced the line of short soft hair down his body. She hesitated at the edge of his briefs, suddenly shy.

'Don't stop now, Marie. Undress me. Touch me,' Rayner demanded hoarsely. With hands that trembled she slowly removed his briefs as he undulated his hips to facilitate their removal. He lay on his back, his magnificent body naked and aroused. 'Show me you're my woman, touch me,' he gratingly reiterated his earlier demand.

Marie leant over him, eating him with her eyes while with a slender hand she tentatively traced the maleness of him. A low groan escaped him and she was intoxicated with the heady sense of her own feminine power. The blood flowed like thick honey through her veins, she felt no fear, only fascination at the perfection of his male form. It was sweet, so very sweet to feel the hard muscular length of him beneath her fingertips. Every nerve-end in her body quivered in a hot fever of response. She stroked him more boldly, he growled deep in his throat and, lost in a sensual daze, she lowered her head and kissed him.

Rayner reacted instantly, his hand grasping the tangled mass of her long red hair, and in a flash their positions were reversed. Marie was swept away on a tide of passionate abandon. She called his name, cried her need, her love, while Rayner kissed her throat, her breast, suckled the hard rosy tips, first one then the other, until she thought she would go mad with the ecstasy of it.

Her body writhed beneath him, her legs entwined with his, and when he finally thrust into her it was like joining in a blazing inferno. Her body of its own volition matched his rhythm instantly. Her fingers dug into the skin of his back as the fiery tension became almost unbearable. She felt a convulsive shudder in his broad shoulders, then a white-hot explosion of tension that obliterated all consciousness.

Marie wasn't sure—maybe she had lost consciousness for a few seconds, with the pure delicious ecstasy of coming together, her quivering body. It was more than she had ever imagined. She felt Rayner's beloved weight on top of her, his sweat-soaked skin, and the deep shudders that racked his huge frame. Tears moistened her eyes at the wonder of it. 'My husband,' she said on a long sigh.

Rayner rolled over on to his back. 'Yes, your husband.' And pulling her half over his prone body he ran his long fingers through the wild glory of her curly hair, scraping it back from her face, his hands holding her head in a fierce grip. 'You, Goldie, are my incredibly sexy little wife, and from this moment on I will be the only man in your bed and in your life. Understand?' he demanded fiercely.

'I understand, my darling,' she murmured, and dismissing the flickering unease his tone had aroused she pressed a soft kiss on the strong column of his throat. The salty taste of his skin was like nectar in her mouth, and slowly she trailed her lips along his jaw-line, gently tracing the harsh scar that marked his handsome face. She had been starved, she was now sated, but lying supine, breast to breast, thigh to thigh, she knew if she lived to be a hundred she would never have enough of this man.

'How did you get the scar, Rayner? You never told me,' she queried softly. She felt so at one with him, lethargic but at the same time exhilarated. She wanted to talk, to share his confidences, every little secret.

'Fighting for my honour. Why, does it offend you?'

Marie felt his strong body tense beneath her, and his hands slid to her shoulders, holding her away from him.

A tender smile curved her love-swollen lips at his hint of vulnerability. 'No, Rayner, never,' she quickly re-assured him. 'I love you, I always have. I remember the first time we made love and I thought it was perfect, but it was so long ago, and tonight... There are no words invented to describe how you made me feel. It was even better than perfect, if that is possible. Was it better for you too?' she asked softly. She did not think she had disappointed him, but as an almost complete novice at making love she needed some reassurance herself.

'My God! I should hope so,' he exclaimed, his sensuous lips twisting in a half-smile, but his eyes weren't laughing. 'I'm surprised you need ask—after all, you are that much older and that much more experienced in the pleasures of the flesh. In fact, I would go so far as to say——' his fingers dug into her shoulders '—my bewitching, salacious little wife, without doubt you are the very best I have ever had,' he opined hardly.

Before her love-hazed eyes, his features tightened into a hard mask. His words were not the romantic avowal she had been looking for, and she stared in puzzlement as he regarded her, his grey eyes glittering with barely controlled anger.

'As for the first time, I seem to remember you cried rape, and I ended up in gaol, hardly something I would want to repeat,' he drawled derisively, and shoving her none too gently away he swung his long legs to the floor and stood up.

'Rayner, no, I...' The past she was not bothered about, but she wanted to tell him he was wrong in his estimation of her, that he was the only man she had ever known, the only man to arouse the sensual side of her nature, but she never got the chance.

Totally unconscious of his nudity he turned, his sensuous mouth twisted in a cynical smile. 'Oh, you might not have used the word rape, but surely that is splitting hairs. I can hear you now, when the policeman asked if I had hurt you, crying, "Yes, yes, he hurt me,"' he taunted in a falsetto voice.

Marie shivered, and suddenly aware of her own nakedness she sat up in the bed, pulling the silk sheet over her chest. She was not cold, but inside an icy finger of fear touched her heart. Rayner's mimicry of her teenage self had finally broken through the rosy afterglow of love she had been wallowing in. Something was wrong, very wrong.

'What, no denial?' he jeered. She raised her head, and every vestige of colour drained from her face as Rayner bent over her, catching her chin with one large hand. His grey eyes gleamed with inimical anger. 'Still using the silent treatment, Goldie?' he grated. 'Well, why not? It's as good as any when you have no defence.' And, with a contemptuous flick of her chin, he let her go.

'Please don't call me Goldie, I prefer Marie,' she said, having finally found her tongue. 'And I don't understand what you mean. I wasn't aware I needed a defence.' She tried to smile, but his obvious anger intimidated her. She reached out her hand to him, grazing his thigh. 'Rayner, we were young and foolish and so we spent the night in gaol. It was unfortunate.' She still shrank with embarrassment every time she remembered the aftermath of their first union, and she could only cringe at her own stupidity in mentioning it tonight, but it had never occurred to her that Rayner had anything to be angry about.

Perhaps if she tried to make light of it... She desperately wanted to placate him. 'It was not so terrible—in a few years' time we will probably laugh with our grandchildren over it,' she offered hopefully, her hand unconsciously stroking softly over his hard thigh.

'My God! You are an insensitive little bitch,' Rayner sneered, and with a savagery she had not thought him capable of he grasped her upper arms and plucked her off the bed, to stand before him. 'No man can laugh at being a prisoner. The brutality, the degradation. You find that amusing?' he snarled, and lowered his head.

His mouth closed over hers with cruel savagery, forcing her lips apart. It was a brutal invasion meant to punish. She was shocked, numbed. Her breasts were crushed against his massive chest and somehow naked, flesh to flesh, her body betrayed her mind, vitally alive in instant response. A whimper escaped her, and Rayner, as though waiting for her surrender, thrust her from him with a harsh, derisory laugh.

'You're right, forget about the past. Now we both have what we want, my wanton little wife,' he drawled, his knowing eyes insolently appraising her slender form, lingering on her hard-tipped breasts.

Marie shivered at the scorn in his voice; she felt humiliated, degraded by his cool appraisal, and suddenly she no longer had any desire to appease him—she was hurting and angry. 'Don't you think you're overreacting slightly, Rayner? After all, one night in gaol hardly makes you an expert on the subject. If anyone has cause to complain surely it should be me,' she said with righteous indignation. 'I was seventeen, terrified out of my wits, and before I knew it I was in the police station with a doctor examining me in the most p-p-personal way p-possible.' She stammered over the words—even now she still hated to remember it, but

Rayner had goaded her into losing her temper, and she smarted at the injustice of it. 'It wasn't surprising I refused to speak. All you had to suffer was a poor night's sleep, while I... The indignity...' she choked.

She tossed back her head, and her topaz eyes shone with tears of anger and frustration. This was her wedding night, and it had all gone terribly wrong. She met Rayner's cold grey eyes, and froze. She had married a stranger. She did not know this man at all.

His hard intent stare played havoc with the last remnants of her self-control and she swallowed, trying to dispel the rising tide of nausea in her stomach. His grey eyes narrowed to mere slits, and the chilling depths seemed to pierce her soul.

'One day? I spent three months in Oxford Prison, mainly because of you,' he said tonelessly, and with a casual gesture he ran his index finger over his jaw. 'That's where I got this scar.'

'Three... No.' The back of her knees touched the edge of the bed and Marie collapsed on to it. She shook her head—it wasn't possible. Tom had promised—her father had said it was a mistake easily corrected. A small fine at worst... Rayner had to be lying. He had to be. But why?

'Yes, ninety days, and every one a lifetime. My cellmates were a clever thief and a man who had murdered his wife. I suppose I should thank you. My friendly thief was a stockbroker, and taught me all I needed to know to start me off on my present career as a financial adviser. Though I didn't feel like thanking you at the time.'

Marie felt the colour drain from her face. His tone of voice, cold and totally without emotion, was more convincing than anger. She believed him. How it had happened she could not begin to understand, but she had no doubt he was telling the truth. His revelation about his occupation barely registered in the shock of realising that Rayner had ended up in gaol because of her. 'I didn't know, I didn't know...' she whispered.

'Cover yourself—you're shivering.' And with a muttered oath he picked up the sheet and draped it around her. Then he casually collected his own towelling robe from a nearby chair and slipped it on, adding, 'I need a shower,' and walked away.

The full implication of his revelation had not truly sunk into her dazed mind, but was hovering on the edge of her consciousness. She was standing on the brink of hell, and somewhere deep, deep down inside she already knew she was going to fall.

'Rayner, wait!' she cried. He stopped about ten feet away from her and turned around. She searched his face for some sign of emotion but there was nothing—his ruggedly handsome features were set in a hard, impenetrable mask.

'What for?' he drawled cynically.

'I really did not know. I left for France the next day. I can't understand how or why—it must have been a mistake.' She was babbling, but she could not help it. 'Tom promised to see to everything. He was calling at the police station before going to London.' She remembered that last day vividly. The argument in the trailer, her father finally agreeing to her mother's taking her away. He could not come with them as he was appearing as the spokesman for the travellers on a late-night television show. It was his big chance, he couldn't miss it, so he arranged to meet up with her mother later in London. Marie had never seen him again. 'He must have fixed everything, he must...' she pleaded, more to herself than Rayner.

'Ah, yes. Your estimable father. I heard he made a very impressive showing on television. Incarcerated as I was at the time, I didn't see it, but I was reliably informed he touched the hearts of many with his impassioned speech on behalf of the travellers' rights to visit Stonehenge. He was a martyr to the cause. His own daughter, a virgin, had been raped by a local landowner's son, and no doubt the villain would be set free. There was one law for the rich and another for the poor. Oh, yes, your father was most eloquent, by all accounts. He certainly fixed things for me,' he concluded with biting cynicism.

'No, there must be some mistake!' she cried desperately, and his mouth twisted in a cruel parody of a smile.

'There was no mistake, believe me. I have the scars to prove it,' he drawled mockingly.

Marie was stunned, shocked senseless. Somewhere she heard a clock chime, and unconsciously counted to twelve. It was the end of her wedding-day. It should have been a cuckoo-clock, she thought irrelevantly. She had obviously been living in cloud cuckoo land. But she still could not quite accept it. 'My father would not have deliberately tried to hurt you.'

'Deliberate or not, he succeeded.' And he turned from her to walk to the bathroom.

For a second she was too shattered to react, then, leaping to her feet, she ran after him, dragging the sheet with her. She caught him at the bathroom door.

'Rayner,' she gripped his arm, 'I didn't know.'

His cold eyes raked her from head to foot, and then there was a slight softening in his expression when he said, 'Now, I believe you didn't know. The only thing I can blame you for is ignorance, and that is no crime. Leave it, Marie—as you said, the past is over and done with, and if you'll excuse me I am finally going to have a shower,' and brushing her aside he opened the door. He hesitated, his hand on the doorknob. 'Get some sleep,

Marie, I won't need you again tonight. I have some business papers to attend to.'

Marie's face turned ashen as if he had struck her. Her eyes stung with unshed tears. The intimacy they had shared meant nothing to him—she meant nothing to him. She could fool herself no longer. He had business to attend to, and yet he had never even bothered to tell her he was no longer a farmer, but a financier. She was of so little importance to him. Whatever his reason was for marrying her, it was not love...

She stumbled across the room and crawled on to the bed, pulling the covers over her shivering body. She fought desperately against the pain and tears. She could not break down, not now. She had to think, to make some kind of sense out of this awful situation.

Her head whirled with a chaotic kaleidoscope of images, feelings, emotions, memories of the past...

Wintering, courtesy of an eccentric farmer, on the outskirts of Whitby, and her first day at school. The warm cosy classroom, her own desk. A hot meal at lunchtime at a proper table, and then playtime. An older girl in the school yard, chanting, 'You're a hippy and you don't wear knickers.'

In her innocence she had retaliated, 'I do so wear knickers,' and, lifting her over-long skirt, had proudly displayed her knee-length Paisley-patterned bloomers with the delicately embroidered lace trim.

Even now she could still hear their cruel laughter as they had proudly displayed their own uniform white panties and jeered at her. She had started to cry, and Miss Dickenson, the headmistress, had consoled her, talking softly, comfortingly, but from that day on she had hated the word 'hippy' and longed to be like everyone else.

Over the years she had learned to ignore the jibes, and with a steely determination she had concentrated on her education. Miss Dickenson had become her friend and mentor. Education opened all doors, and the young Goldie had believed it. She had been a grade A student all the way through school, in spite of the fact that she always missed the summer term. Every spring her parents set off on the travellers' trail heading for the south of England and Stonehenge for the summer solstice in June.

Marie stirred restlessly on the wide bed. Stonehenge, the setting for the most wonderful moment of her life and also the worst. How many other people's lives had it affected over the centuries? she mused. A huge circle of standing stones, an ancient prehistoric monument, temple of the Druids even today. The original earthwork was constructed in about 2800 BC, and according to some scientists it had been added to and in use for almost seventeen centuries until after 1100 BC.

She remembered the first time she'd seen it; there had only been a few people there at the time, and she had gazed in awe at the rising sun framed between two large sarsen stones over five and a half metres high. But by the time she was sixteen she hadn't cared if she never saw the place again.

She had pleaded with her parents to allow her to stay at school for the summer term and take her final exams, but to no avail. Eventually Miss Dickenson had solved the problem by arranging for her to take them in the following November, when other people would be doing resits.

So, still smarting with resentment, she had trailed off to Salisbury Plain, and some miles from Stonehenge they had camped on Rayner's father's land. He'd spoken to her and she'd been smitten. He'd become the focus of all her adolescent fantasies, and on midsummer nights she'd never gone near Stonehenge but had stayed in the trailer dreaming of Rayner.

Afterwards she'd listened to her father raging about the police presence, but never payed much attention. In the November she'd taken her exams and passed them all, and to her delight had got a live-in job as a trainee receptionist in a small hotel in Whitby.

The following year she'd once again been on the road. Tom, at his manipulative best, had persuaded her.

Marie rolled over on to her stomach and buried her face in the pillow. With brutal honesty she admitted to herself that Tom's pleading would never have convinced her on its own, but deep down inside she had nurtured a secret hope, a desire to see the young Rayner again.

They had arrived early at the beginning of June, and to her delight she'd bumped into Rayner in Salisbury town. He'd recognised her immediately and taken her to an old-fashioned tea-shop for coffee and cake, then insisted on driving her back to the camp-site.

She'd been in heaven, but as it drew nearer to the twenty-first of June everything had changed. A large convoy of travellers had been stopped by the police. Suddenly the media had been much in evidence, and what had always been a reasonably controlled event had suddenly become a national incident.

She'd met Rayner once more in a quiet copse of trees some half a mile from the camp. He had confided to her that this was the last time the travellers would be allowed to camp on his father's land. It was causing too much trouble. Goldie had realised he was right. The countryside around was crawling with all sorts of people, and very few of them genuine travellers but unemployed youngsters, punks with pink hair, fringe groups of activists wanting to get in on the act.

By the time midsummer night arrived she had been thoroughly depressed and frightened. The police had set up roadblocks, and stopped everyone fifteen miles from the monument, which unfortunately happened to be only about a mile from where they were camped. She'd been swept up in a wild surge of people about a thousand strong, fighting with the police. Eventually she had managed to push her way out of the crowd, and, battered and bruised, she had sought the sanctuary of the woods, and it was there once again she'd met Rayner.

He had held her in his arms to comfort her; they could hear the noise in the distance but, locked in their own little world of growing sensual awareness, they had ignored it.

Marie groaned into the pillow as she remembered the rest. Rayner's lovemaking had been everything she had ever imagined—no young girl could have had a better initiation to sex—but when he had laughed and said, 'A hippy! Wait till I tell my father,' she had been brutally disillusioned—she did not hear the rest of his words. In her pain her hand had found a piece of wood and, jumping to her feet, she had struck out at him, crying hysterically. The sudden beam of a torch had pierced the darkness, outlining her struggling form and Rayner with the stick he had wrenched from her in his hand.

Looking back now, she could see it had been an improbable set of circumstances that had led to what happened next. There were two policemen; one had tackled Rayner and the other had asked if she was hurt, and she had cried yes, before a lifetime of being wary of the police had struck her dumb.

She had been terrified during the drive in the car to the police station in Salisbury. People had been milling around all over, and the police had made over a hundred arrests in the riot that had occurred over Stonehenge—

her father one of them. He'd stared at her bedraggled state, her blood-stained dress, and before she knew what had happened she'd been bundled into a small room. She could still hear her father's voice demanding she be examined...

She had refused to speak—she just wanted to hide in a corner and die. The police surgeon had given her a sedative and the charges against her father had been dropped so he could take her home.

She had awoken the next afternoon to hear Tom and her mother talking, and that was when she'd finally realised Rayner had been charged with assaulting a police officer. Stunned, she'd listened to the conversation. Tom had been furious and swore bitterly that Rayner should be made to pay for raping his daughter, never mind some small offence of striking a policeman—something a man in Rayner's position would have no trouble wriggling out of. No—Goldie must make a statement to the police, and her mother must take her along to the police station to do so. He had to leave for London and his television interview. Michelle would just have to keep off the drugs for a couple of days and look after her daughter.

In that moment Goldie had realised just how little she'd meant to her father. Believing as he had that she had been raped, his causes had still come first...

Bluntly she'd told her parents she had not been raped, but had been a willing party to the act, and in the ensuing argument she'd finally got rid of all her pent-up anger and resentment. She'd extracted a promise from Tom that he would explain the circumstances to the police, then Rayner's angry outburst would not seem so bad.

Finally Tom had convinced her there was no chance of Rayner going to gaol for punching the policeman; the worst that could happen was a stiff fine, or a suspended sentence. As for Michelle, she had really surprised Goldie. She could hear her mother's voice now...

'Marigold, I'm sorry, so sorry. I never realised you felt that way, but now, if it's not too late, I'm going to put everything right for you.'

And she had. After a boat trip and a long drive, Marie had been introduced to a grandfather she had never known existed, and a whole new way of life...

CHAPTER FIVE

SOMEWHERE in the distance a clock struck one. Marie's head was pounding, and her eyes smarted with unshed tears—she dashed them away angrily with the back of her hand, and reaching out she switched off the bedside light. Only a slim door separated her from Rayner and there was no way she wanted him to see or hear that she was upset. She had learned at a very early age to hide her tears, and the lesson came to her aid now.

Rayner's earlier comments echoed in her head, and his cold dismissal—'I won't need you again tonight'—brought a stab of pain to her heart, but still she refused to analyse his words.

Later...tomorrow, perhaps! She was too tired, she told herself. Her lips twisted in a bitter, derisory smile—who was she kidding? There was no likelihood of her going to sleep.

Her body felt heavy with fatigue, but it was the crushing sense of her own guilt that really weighed her down; remembering the past was just a way of delaying facing up to the present. Three months in gaol... She could not understand it. Surely Tom must have explained—assaulting a police officer, under the circumstances, could not warrant a custodial sentence, could it? She didn't know...

The door opened and Rayner entered the bedroom. Marie heard him curse as he knocked against a chair, then the mattress depressed beneath his weight, and she felt the cool air on her body as he pulled back the covers and lay down beside her.

She thought of pretending to be asleep, but, thinking clearly for the first time in hours, she dismissed the idea. The strength of mind that had seen her through school against all the odds, then helped her adapt to a foreign country and her grandfather's way of life, gave her the courage to speak.

'Rayner, we have to talk.'

His arms reached for her, and her body tensed against the strength of his muscular frame.

'I can think of better things to do,' he drawled throatily, his hand stroking down to her slender hips, drawing her closer to his hard thighs.

Heat rushed through her body, and for a moment she wanted to give in to her traitorous senses, but her mind was filled with too many questions. 'You said you didn't need me again tonight,' she reminded him bluntly.

'So I was wrong,' he husked, his breath hot against her throat.

'No, Rayner,' she said, forcing herself to reject the sensuous delight his very masculine body offered.

Abruptly he withdrew and, sitting up, switched on the light. 'Refusing me already. That must be some kind of record for newly-weds.' He turned slightly and his cold eyes mocked her cynically. 'So talk.'

There was so much she wanted to know she didn't know where to begin, and lying next to him in the wide bed was hardly the best place for a serious conversation. It made her vulnerable. She glanced up at him—he looked like some Eastern potentate, his arms crossed over his bare chest, his expression forbidding. She had the fanciful thought that he could be passing judgement on some lesser mortal, and any moment he would give the thumbs-down.

The silence lengthened uncomfortably, tightening her already overstretched nerves. She breathed deeply and burst into speech. 'I know we agreed to forget about the past, and it was stupid of me to ask...before——' she hesitated '—well, what I did. You had every right to be angry. Three months is a long time. But what I can't understand is—why such a sentence? It seems totally unfair.'

A harsh laugh escaped him. 'My, such concern,' he mocked. 'Unfortunately, seven years too late. Why, my dear, does it upset your conventional little mind to find you have married a man with a criminal record?'

'But how——?' she began.

He did not let her finish the sentence, his handsome face twisted with rage. 'How?' he snarled, turning on his side to stare down at her. 'Because a certain young lady and her mother skipped the country.' He reminded her of her headlong flight to France, and Marie winced inwardly at his stinging sarcasm. 'In ordinary circumstances I would have spent a night in gaol and have been in front of the magistrate the next day, but there was nothing ordinary about the night I was arrested,' he opined bitterly, his angry gaze unwavering on her pale face.

For the life of her, Marie could not break the contact, and she listened in mounting horror as he continued with an icy, controlled deliberation that made her blood run cold.

'The small gaol in Salisbury was overflowing with travellers arrested for causing a riot. A bus was provided, and a number of us were shipped to Oxford Prison, the nearest place with any cell-space. When I finally appeared in front of the magistrate thirty-six hours later, the police inspector opposed bail on the charge of assaulting a police officer because they had, and I quote, "a reasonable suspicion that a more serious charge might follow after completing further inquiries,'' unquote. After Tom's outburst on television, no one was in any doubt what the more serious charge would be. Rape, my dear Goldie.'

'Oh, God!' Marie whispered—it was worse than she had imagined.

'By the time my father's solicitor, a nice old man from Winchester, but totally inept at criminal law, finally got around to appealing the next week against the no-bail decision, the court was informed that certain articles of clothing had been sent to the Home Office Forensic Laboratory, and the police were awaiting the result. In addition, as your trailer was on my land, if released I might have attempted to interfere with prospective witnesses.'

'But we weren't even there,' Marie blurted.

'But you were expected back—for the police "reasonable suspicion" is a very handy tool. The following week, when the bail hearing was held yet again, I was not there myself. Instead I was in the prison hospital as, by that time, I had had a fight with a rather nasty character, whose sexual predilection was for blond young men.'

'Oh, no...'

'Don't look so shocked, Marie. I defended my honour, hence the scar.'

But at what cost? she thought, staring at his harsh face. Now she understood...and she was filled with a heart-deep sadness for the young man she had once known. She listened to him, barely registering what he was saying, it was just too much to take in.

'British justice is probably the best in the world, but it's not perfect. At the third hearing, my solicitor informed me, the police had completed the case of assault, and it had been entered on the court list. He was quite pleased about it, the old fool. He happily informed me that I had been remanded in custody until the trial, but not to worry, the trial could be at just twenty-four hours' notice. Unfortunately for me I was not that lucky. I waited in a prison cell a further nine weeks. Finally the case came to court. I was given ninety days for assault, but as I had already served that amount of time I was released.

'The Press had a field day with the policeman's evidence on the circumstances of my arrest. Most people thought I had been very lucky to get away with ninety days—even the judge informed me that I was a very lucky man that I wasn't before him for a much more *serious offence*.'

His hand snaked out, capturing her throat, pushing her head back into the pillow, his thumb and forefinger caressing her skin with a barely controlled pressure. She stared into his eyes with growing fear. 'Please let go,' she said weakly.

'Never.' The word was a threat. His lips curled in a chilling smile. 'I haven't finished. You wouldn't want me to leave out the most relevant part, now, would you?' he sneered. 'Every single morning of those three months, I woke up with the thought: today Goldie will turn up and tell them it was a mistake. My father even hired a detective to try and find you. Finally, as I walked into the dock with the spectre of being charged with rape still hanging over me, and years in gaol a very real possibility, I realised how completely you had betrayed me.' His hand tightened on her throat. 'If I had found you, I'd have strangled you. Then a week later I read of the accident in Turkey.' His hand relaxed slightly, and he stared down at her flushed, frightened face. 'I thought you were dead.'

Dead; he had wished her dead. The colour drained from her face. It was worse, much worse than she had thought possible. Her mind confusedly jumbled his words. If she had betrayed him, it had been an unconscious betrayal. She felt his fingers on her throat. 'Please, you're hurti——' She stopped. How she must have hurt him...

She saw his expression change, and thought she saw a kind of tenderness in his cold grey eyes, but it was gone as quickly as it had come. His mouth twisted in a bitter, self-derisory smile.

'God! I told myself I was glad...and cried...' His dark head swooped, his mouth covering hers in a brutal kiss.

Marie, frozen in shocked horror, offered no resistance as his mouth ravaged hers. His hand stroked from her throat to cup the creamy fullness of her breast, and her mind rebelled even as her body responded.

He loomed over her, large and somehow menacing, the cover was pushed to her feet, and his eyes raked her nudity with a glittering ruthlessness, a violence fiercely controlled.

'Don't, please don't.' She raised her hands to his chest, her whole body trembling. She knew if he took her in anger it would be the end of all her dreams.

'Yes,' he said thickly, 'I have to—an exorcism, if you like.' He lowered his body, trapping her beneath him with insulting ease. His mouth covered hers, and she could taste the rage in his kiss.

She struggled, fighting the surge of desire that threatened to melt her bones. He went on kissing her, parting her lips, thrusting deeply, while his hands roamed at will over her quivering flesh. She felt a dizzying weakness wash over her as his passionate lovemaking fuelled her growing desire.

'You want me. Say it, Marie...' He rasped the words against her skin.

When his fair head moved down her body, his mouth hot on the rigid peak of her breast, she was lost. 'I want you, I want you,' she moaned, and arched against him, a wild savage excitement sweeping her along.

A guttural sound of triumph rumbled deep in his throat. He was fully aroused and with a single aggressive thrust he took possession of her. It was a quick, shatteringly ecstatic release. Marie lay, eyes closed, her body quivering in the aftermath of passion, but a coldness slowly stole over her heart as reality intruded.

Rayner slumped against her, his harsh breathing sounding loud in the silence of the room. She carefully slithered from under him, and he made no attempt to restrain her but, raising himself on one elbow, lay on his side, watching her.

Slowly she sat up, pulling the cover up over her breasts. She felt like an old woman. 'You hate me, don't you?' she said softly, fighting back the tears; she could fool herself no longer. 'I can't think why you married me,' she choked.

'Don't be ridiculous, Marie. It wasn't hate you experienced in my arms a few moments ago... The sexual chemistry between us is explosive, always was. Some things never change.'

Chemistry, yes, Marie thought sadly, but love, no. It was some darker emotion that motivated Rayner, she was sure of it...

She tensed as he ran a taunting hand down over her naked thigh. 'I married you because I want you. You have a beautiful body.' His long fingers strayed to her inner thigh. She shivered. 'And, I am beginning to think, an endless capacity for enjoyment,' he opined lazily, aware of her instant reaction to his intimate touch.

'And is that the only reason?' she asked, and helpless to stop she added, 'What about love?'

'Love is a state of mind women like you think themselves into, to justify indulging their natural sexual appetite with a man, and afterwards they just as quickly think themselves out of it,' he declared hardly. Restlessly he flung back the covers and got out of bed and, his back to her, he donned his robe. Then he slowly turned to look down into her wide, moisture-filled eyes. 'Don't look so crushed, Marie. We all have to grow up some time, and you've had a longer childhood than most,' he said scathingly.

She swallowed the lump in her throat as the knife twisted in her heart, and she clenched her teeth in an effort to subdue the pain. 'I thought you loved...' she murmured almost to herself—never in her life had she felt such anguish. She looked up at him, and it was as if she were seeing him for the first time. No, not quite. She was reminded of their meeting at the château. She had thought then he was a stranger, his grey eyes as hard as flint. His face held the same expression now.

'I don't recall mentioning love.' He smiled and his lips parted to reveal predatory white teeth. 'You've lived in a dream world for years, seeing only what you wanted to see. It's way past time you faced up to reality, Marie darling.'

She cringed at his contemptuously drawled endearment, and suddenly she was angry, at Rayner, but mostly with herself for being so incredibly, foolishly naïve. She hated to admit it, but there was some truth in his words.

'I don't think I like your reality, Rayner. You may not have lied to me, but you certainly have lied by omission. I thought you...' Loved me, she was going to say, but stopped, pride holding back the words. Frantically searching her mind, she clumsily came up with his earlier casual revelation. 'W-w-were a farmer, and tonight I find out you are a financier.' She laughed, a hard, brittle sound. 'My God, I don't even know where we were supposed to live. Do you still have the farm?'

'Not "were"...."will".' His words cut across her harshly. 'And yes, I do still have the farm, and it *will* be our home.'

She watched him walk into the bathroom, and closed her eyes to hold back the tears.

'Nothing has changed, Marie.'

She opened her eyes and stared at him accusingly. 'Maybe not for you, but for me. You tricked me into marrying you.' The pieces of the jigsaw were beginning to fit in her tired mind. He didn't love her, never had. It was obvious, now she understood his anger. He wanted revenge, he blamed her for being in prison.

He sat down on the bed, and she knew he was about to touch her again. She raised her hands to ward him off, and he grasped her wrists, pinning them to the bed.

'I did not trick you,' he denied, pushing her back against the pillows. 'You did that all by yourself, my sweet wife. Any time in the past month you could have asked me anything you liked, but you were so tied up in your own little dream world you never bothered. Frankly I was amazed at your total lack of curiosity.' He gave her a lazy, mocking smile, reached up and flicked her hair back from her shoulders. 'It is an unusual trait in a woman, but one that suited me perfectly,' he said silkily.

She knocked his hand away. 'I just bet it did,' she responded, unable to hide the bitterness from her voice, realising he must have cold-bloodedly planned to marry her from the start. But something didn't make sense. If he'd thought she was dead, how? How had he done it?

A coincidence? Hardly... 'Tell me, Rayner. Was it just chance that brought you to my home?' She had to know it all, however much it humiliated her.

'Yes, oddly enough it was, in a way.' He sat back, his hands behind him on the bed, supporting his weight. He looked down at her, his grey eyes gleaming with mocking amusement.

'How?' she asked, controlling her anger at him. 'And why?'

'Well, I suppose you deserve the truth. All the books say there should be complete honesty between man and wife.' His lips twitched slightly. 'Who am I to argue?'

Marie glanced up at him with fury in her eyes. He was laughing at her, the swine, and she ached to knock the triumphant smirk off his face, only fear of what he would do in return stilled her hand. 'Get on with it,' she gritted. She was hanging on to her control by a thread, but she had to have her suspicions confirmed, to know the worst. Then perhaps she could come to terms with this disastrous night.

As though sensing how near she was to the edge, Rayner, in a voice devoid of any discernible emotion, began to speak.

'Last June I was in Deauville for the weekend. Stuck in a traffic jam, I saw you walking along the street. You looked like Goldie, but I knew it couldn't be. Then by chance some tourist stopped you to ask directions, only a couple of feet from my car. You replied in perfect English, and that was it.'

She had been staying with Uncle Jacques in June— that was the reason she had not gone again in the August with her grandpapa.

'I followed you, you got in a red car, and the trail led to Jacques's stud farm. I intended to follow you up the next day. I was intrigued as to how the young Goldie could turn into a chic, poised Frenchwoman.' He paused slightly, his face taut and cynical. 'Unfortunately I had to return to England immediately the next morning—my father had suffered another stroke.'

Marie knew his father was dead. When she had asked for the names of the people who he wanted to invite to the wedding, he had told her he had no family and, as for his friends, a party in England later would be more appropriate. But she'd never realised his father's death had been so recent.

'An investigative journalist acquaintance of mine did some checking for me, and came up with the information about you and your family.'

'All my family?' she interjected, horrified at the thought of someone spying on them.

'Don't worry, Marie, my friend would never betray a confidence—your ladylike image is perfectly safe,' he said sardonically, before continuing coldly, 'After my father died in July, I thought it would be interesting to look you up. Relive old times. I bought a couple of horses from a friend, and came over to Jacques's stud farm. You know the rest. I met you, wanted you, married you, and you were delightfully eager. Satisfied?' he prompted with mocking triumph.

'Satisfied, no. Horrified, yes.' Marie stared at him in disbelief. He made it sound so cold, so calculated, and, to her own shame, so easy. 'But why marriage?' Her voice cracked on the last word, and she knew she could not retain control of her emotions much longer, but he still wasn't telling her the whole truth.

'Many reasons.' His voice was crisp, matter-of-fact. 'I'm thirty-one years old, tired of playing the field. I need a hostess in my home, and I promised my father before he died that I would marry and produce an heir to continue the family name. It seemed the least I could do for him, after ruining the last few years of his life.' He said it so calmly, Marie wasn't sure she had heard him correctly.

'Ruin his life? I can't believe that,' she muttered.

'Mud sticks.' He spoke suddenly and with great bitterness. 'My father was an honourable man, well liked in the county. What do you think it did to him, having his only son in prison, and everyone in the county speculating on whether I was a rapist or not?'

His eyes held hers with a look of such contempt, she wanted to hide her face, but she couldn't. 'I can't imagine,' she said in a horrified whisper, hardly aware she had spoken. She was mesmerised, watching him as he continued.

'Once I returned home it became obvious. The dinner parties where the men would arrive with pathetic excuses for the absence of their daughters, and in some cases their wives. A policeman calling at my home to check my whereabouts a particular evening. A sex crime in the area and they came straight to my door. After the second such call I packed up and went to London and started my career as a financial adviser.' He straightened up suddenly and bent forward, his hands once more either side of her legs.

Marie was stunned. The picture he had drawn was a hundred times worse than anything she had imagined. Her eyes widened in distress. Rayner had been a proud young man; how it must have hurt him, and his father... Compassion stirred within her, and impulsively she sat up in bed and reached out a slender hand. 'I'm sorry,' she husked, the words totally inadequate to describe the depths of her regret.

'There is nothing to be sorry about.' His mouth twisted in a cynical smile, and straightening up he grasped the hand she offered, turning it palm up in his own. 'Your hand in my life turned me into a millionaire.' He raised his head, so she could see the glittering hardness in his eyes. 'On the other hand,' he sneered, 'your father I will never forgive. His outburst on the television destroyed my father's pride in his only son, and blackened the name of Millard in front of the whole country. After I was released from prison I intended suing him, but he died first.'

Marie was too shattered to react, and for long moments she stared up into his harsh face, not wanting to believe what she was hearing. But Rayner had no need to lie. Tom had appeared on television and accused Rayner, and in doing so had betrayed her trust as well, deliberately using his own daughter to further his cause; and, Marie finally admitted to herself, her fanatical father had been more than capable of such an action.

With blinding clarity she saw it all. She closed her eyes to mask the pain, the death of all her dreams. Slowly she opened her eyes. She glanced at his strong hand still holding hers, she felt the sensuous warmth of flesh against flesh. His expertise as a lover she knew, but looking once again into his icy grey eyes she recognised he had a heart as cold as stone.

'You planned this all along, Rayner. Some kind of spiteful revenge. The sins of the father and all that...' Her voice shook with the force of her emotion. 'When I think of what we did earlier, I want to be sick.' And it was true; she had lost all inhibition, given everything of herself to this man, and she did not know him at all. 'Well, I hope you were satisfied, because I will never allow you to touch me again.' She pulled her hand free and slid across the bed to jump out of the other side. She could not stand his proximity a moment longer. 'I will sleep next door on the sofa.' She had to get out of the room.

'Don't be so melodramatic, Marie. It doesn't suit you,' he opined hardly, his cold gaze raking her naked form. 'Apart from being blatantly untrue. You wanted me before and you will again. Celibacy is not your style, my dear. I could take you in my arms now, and in minutes you would be begging me for it,' he said crudely. 'As for sleeping next door, forget it. You are my wife and you will share my bed until I decide otherwise.'

She picked her négligé off the floor and pulled it on, knowing full well it was futile—the garment was transparent. She turned and stared at him, and found herself looking into a stranger's eyes which were observing her with a frightening intensity. Panic rose within her and it took all her self-control to remain calm. 'Don't hold your breath waiting,' she snapped. 'No doubt you enjoyed setting me up, letting me think . . . Never mind, I've had enough.'

'For tonight, maybe,' he inserted mockingly, and with a casualness that she could only envy he shrugged off his robe and slid into bed. 'Now get in here, and don't be so childish. You need have no fear of my touching you. I have never forced myself on a woman in my life, I *always* ask first, as you should know better than most,' he said derisively.

Marie flushed with shame at his timely reminder, and hated him for making her feel guilty. Now she understood why earlier he had held back even in the white-hot heat of passion, insisting she tell him out loud of her want and need. He had to have the words. Their youthful experience had scarred him more deeply than she could ever have believed.

Her own inherent honesty forced her to acknowledge that some of the blame must be hers. She had given to her father a message for the police that she had been too cowardly to deliver herself, and because of that one small act she had ended up seven years later married to a man who did not love her.

She was unaware of how plainly her confused emotions were reflected on her beautiful expressive features. Her gaze strayed over his recumbent form, lying with the sheet pulled loosely across his waist, the dark gold hair of his chest gleaming in the subdued lighting. She wryly acknowledged that here was a man whom no right-minded woman would refuse, but for the sake of her own self-respect she would have to.

'No,' she said softly, finally shaking her head. With one word, she was denying her love and all her dreams. Contrary to what he thought, she was a realist, and there was no way she could endure a loveless marriage—better to make the break quick and clean. 'Tomorrow I will find a lawyer.' She closed her eyes briefly. 'This was a ghastly mistake.'

Rayner slowly unfurled from the bed, gloriously naked, and walked across the space dividing them. She wanted to turn and run, but she had done that once before with disastrous consequences. It was time to stand up for herself. Bravely she faced him.

He grasped her shoulders, and his voice was hard, fierce with repressed anger. 'I've had enough of your bloody histrionics for one night. You wanted to talk, and we've talked. If you didn't like what you heard, tough... Today you made solemn promises to me in front of all your family and friends, and I am holding you to them. There will be no talk of lawyers or separation. You are my wife, and, when you get over indulging in childish fantasies of love, you will admit you are getting exactly what you want from this marriage, just as much as I am.'

Love...a childish fantasy. He actually believed that, Marie realised, and for a second she almost felt sorry for him, until he continued.

'Contrary to what you think, I'm not looking for revenge. The sexual chemistry between us is intense. If I had wanted revenge I would have turned down flat what you so freely offered.' He seized her hand as she raised it to strike him, the conceit of the man infuriating her. 'No, we will not go through all that again. For once you will listen to me.' He was watching her closely as a hawk might watch its prey. 'I admit one of the reasons for marrying you was because it suited my sense of justice, and, because of that, there can be no divorce. Do you understand?'

A vivid image of Rayner dining at her home flashed in her mind. He had worn exactly the same expression then, when he had told her the meaning of his name—Warrior of Judgement. She had brushed away the odd premonition she had felt at the time. God! How he must have laughed at her! He was right in one respect: she had only seen what she wanted to see... At last she understood perfectly; all the pieces finally fitted.

'Yes, I'm not a fool, even though I have behaved like one for the past month,' she said bitterly. 'A loveless marriage of convenience is perfect for someone so lacking in feeling as you. The only thing that still amazes me is that you are actually egotistical enough to imagine that I would find any satisfaction in such an arrangement,' she said derisively.

He slid one strong hand slowly down her arm to catch her much smaller hand in his, and deliberately he raised it to his lips. His smoky eyes lit with mocking triumph as he kissed her fingertips. A surge of heat flowed through her body, and suddenly she was intensely aware of his naked form only inches from her own; the air between them once more crackled with sexual tension.

'You will find more than enough satisfaction—in every way,' he said silkily. 'I know you better than you know yourself, Marie. All you have ever wanted was a home and respectability, money and status. By marrying me you have acquired all those things.' His tongue licked lightly over her palm, and she sucked in her breath at the sensation, not quick enough to hide her reaction from him. 'Plus the added advantage of great sexual compatibility. What more could any woman want?' he declared, a self-satisfied smile curving his firm lips at her obvious response.

Marie flinched at his callous summing-up of her character. 'I had all that at my grandfather's house. I didn't have to marry you for it,' she declared her eyes flaring with anger, mostly directed at herself for being so easily duped. She wished he would put some clothes on—his unashamed nakedness intimidated her.

Rayner's hands tightened on her shoulder and wrist, and Marie suddenly sensed a change in him—he was no longer so in control. 'Not quite, my dear. In France you would always have been known as the bastard granddaughter of Henri.' Marie's face paled as if he had struck her. 'Now you have a legal name—Mrs Millard—and you will keep it. Because, no matter what I do, you could not stand the shame of returning to your grandfather's house and admitting failure. No, I think I can safely say you will do as you're told and return to England with me. In no time at all you will become a leading light in the community—with your poise and elegance, it's inevitable. And as for your sex life, I won't question how you have managed before, but I can assure you I am more than capable of keeping you satisfied in that department. All you have to do is ask,' he concluded cynically.

There was a silence that seemed to go on forever. Marie had felt each word like the lash of a whip. The pain was terrible; she would never forget this moment, she thought hollowly. All night she had battled with the knowledge that he did not care for her, but somehow, somewhere, a tiny thread of hope had lingered. But no more. With each word he had made his opinion of her plain. He saw her as a shallow, status-seeking woman, and the horrible part was that in one respect he was correct. She could not go back to her grandfather, she could not bear to appear less than perfect in the old man's eyes. She turned away.

'I won't ask,' she said quietly, and, her hand on the door, she looked back at him, her topaz eyes wide and dulled with pain. 'Not ever! As for the rest, you're probably right. Now if you will excuse me, tonight I need some privacy.' The sofa was a hundred times more inviting than Rayner's bed, and she did not think she could stand to be near him a moment longer.

He stepped a little closer, a flash of some emotion in his grey eyes, but Marie was too blinded by tears to see. 'Come to bed, Marie, it has been a long day and an even longer night.' He reached out his hand to her.

She brushed it aside, but she could not speak. She wanted to cry out that he was wrong about her, but a sick suspicion held her back. Perhaps, just perhaps he was right...

'If you want to play the martyr and sleep on the sofa, go ahead. But ruffled feathers make a cold blanket, Marie.' His deep voice mocked her, but she ignored it and walked out of the room, quietly closing the door behind her.

PLAY
HARLEQUIN'S

LUCKY HEARTS
GAME

AND YOU COULD GET

- ★ FREE BOOKS
- ★ A FREE 20″ NECKLACE
- ★ A FREE SURPRISE GIFT
- ★ AND MUCH MORE

TURN THE PAGE AND
DEAL YOURSELF IN →

PLAY "LUCKY HEARTS" AND YOU COULD GET...

★ Exciting Harlequin Presents® novels—FREE
★ A 20″ Necklace—FREE
★ A surprise mystery gift that will delight you—FREE

THEN CONTINUE YOUR LUCKY STREAK WITH A SWEETHEART OF A DEAL

When you return the postcard on the opposite page, we'll send you the books and gifts you qualify for, absolutely free! Then you'll get 6 new Harlequin Presents® novels every month, delivered right to your door months before they're available in stores. If you decide to keep them, you'll pay only $2.49* per book—that's a saving of 30¢ off the cover price. And there's no extra charge for postage and handling! You can cancel at any time by marking "cancel" on your statement or returning a shipment to us at our cost.

Free Newsletter!

You'll get a free newsletter—an insider's look at our most popular authors and their upcoming novels.

Special Extras—Free!

When you subscribe to the Harlequin Reader Service®, you'll also get additional free gifts from time to time as a token of our appreciation for being a home subscriber.

You'll look like a million dollars when you wear this elegant necklace! It's a generous 20 inches long and each link is double-soldered for strength and durability.

HARLEQUIN'S

With a coin — scratch off the silver card and check below to see how many gifts you get.

YES! I have scratched off the silver card. Please send me all the books and gifts for which I qualify. I understand that I am under no obligation to purchase any books, as explained on the opposite page.

106 CIH AEFW (U-H-P-02/92)

NAME

ADDRESS   APT.

CITY   STATE   ZIP

DETACH AND MAIL CARD TODAY

DETACH AND MAIL CARD TODAY

BUSINESS REPLY MAIL
FIRST CLASS MAIL   PERMIT NO. 717   BUFFALO, NY

POSTAGE WILL BE PAID BY ADDRESSEE

HARLEQUIN READER SERVICE
3010 WALDEN AVE
PO BOX 1867
BUFFALO NY 14240-9952

NO POSTAGE
NECESSARY
IF MAILED
IN THE
UNITED STATES

Blinded by a rush of bitter tears, she leaned against the closed door, and fought desperately to control them. Choking back a sob, she crossed the wide expanse of deep rose carpet and collapsed on the large, ten-cushioned velvet sofa. She curled her bare feet up under her and laid her head back against the soft cushions. She glanced around the beautiful room she had entered only hours before as a blushing, ecstatic bride full of hope for the future. Where had it all gone? her foolish heart cried.

It was her wedding night and she was alone... A low, anguished moan escaped her; for one short day she had been truly happy. Rayner's lovemaking had transported her to the stars and for a brief, wonderful moment she had touched heaven. Then one careless comment and her world had crashed around her unsuspecting head.

It had been an illusion, and Rayner had shattered it with the truth. She battled against the pain of knowing that to Rayner she would never be anything but the girl who had betrayed him. Even if he now believed she knew nothing about his imprisonment, she was still the daughter of a man who definitely had betrayed him...

She pulled her flimsy robe tight around her shivering body, and cast a quick glance around the room, looking for some form of cover. She saw Rayner's cashmere overcoat flung carelessly on a chair and, rising, she walked over and collected it. Returning to the sofa she huddled down and pulled the coat over her slender body.

The familiar scent of Rayner, spicy and all male, clung to the fabric, tormenting her senses, but somehow comforting. It was silly, she knew; she had to pull herself together and think rationally. So far she had just been reacting. Now, she must decide what to do.

Looking back over the past few weeks she could see clearly now what had been a glaring truth all along.

Rayner cared nothing for her. She had been like an ostrich with its head in the sand, believing only what she wanted to believe. In that respect Rayner had been right.

The first day, when she had seen him from her bedroom window, she had been frightened and panic-stricken, sure he was trouble... She should have trusted her first impression and acted accordingly. Instead she had adopted a cool air of quiet confidence, and at the first opportunity she had politely asked him not to mention the past.

When he had agreed so readily she had jumped at his offer of friendship, all her fear forgotten. That very same evening he had made love to her and, worse, questioned her morals, but she had quickly accepted his feeble explanation of a joke. A few passionate moments in his arms and immediately she had succumbed to his sexual expertise, humiliatingly eager to take him at face value, believing what he wanted her to believe.

She realised now that he actually did think she was a promiscuous woman. Perhaps that was no bad thing, she thought wryly, at least he would never know what a complete idiot she had been. For years she had repressed the sensuous side of her nature, and when Rayner had taken her in his arms she had gone up in flames, and the next day at Les Sables d'Olonne he had made love to her.

He had been clever, very clever—once he was certain of her response, he had not kissed her again for almost a week. He was a manipulating swine, she thought bitterly.

It was so obvious to her now—his hand on her thigh or an arm around her shoulders, a quick hug, just enough to keep her in a perpetual state of sexual tension, until the last day of his stay. In retrospect she could not believe how dense she had been.

At La Lanterne, in La Rochelle, with the ghosts of a thousand prisoners, Rayner had virtually given himself away, and still she had not questioned his motives—instead she had agreed with embarrassing speed to his marriage proposal.

She stirred restlessly on her makeshift bed. Rayner had said she lived in a dream world, and she could not blame him for thinking that, after the way she had behaved. Unfortunately for a few short weeks she had lived in a fairy-tale of her own making. She could only conclude she must have suffered a brainstorm, a mental aberration of some kind, a regression back to her teenage years. There was no other explanation for her humiliatingly naïve behaviour.

She turned on to her stomach, burying her face in the cushion. Realising the enormous extent of her folly did nothing to ease her aching heart, or help find a solution to her present predicament.

She burnt with shame at her earlier uninhibited, almost aggressive lovemaking. She had behaved like a sex-starved fool, and Rayner had encouraged her, urging her on to every kind of liberty, even demanding the words, and she had willingly declared her love. While all the time he had been indulging his lust. It could not be anything else, she knew that now. He must have been gloating at how easily he had duped her...

CHAPTER SIX

A KISS as light as thistledown on her soft lips woke Marie from a dreamless sleep. Slowly she opened her eyes, a beauteous smile curving her mouth, lighting tiny sparks of gold in her topaz eyes as she gazed up into the handsome face of her husband. Then like a douche of ice-water the events of the previous night surfaced in her mind, and her eyelids instinctively lowered to mask the pain.

'Sleeping Beauty, awakened by a kiss,' Rayner mocked. 'Romantic enough for you, hmm?'

Her smile gone, she swung her legs to the floor and rose to her feet. 'Romance has no part in our relationship,' she responded coldly. 'If you'll excuse me, I'm going to have a shower.' She could not face him, not yet ...

As she would have brushed past him, Rayner caught her arm in a steely grip. 'Look at me, Marie.'

Slowly she raised her head, meeting and holding his gaze, and she swallowed as he gently brushed his fingers along the shadows under her eyes. 'Why?' She had to say something or she would break down and cry.

He looked devastatingly attractive, his silver hair, still damp from the shower, lay dark against his broad forehead. The clean spicy scent of him filled her nostrils. He was immaculately dressed; the grey silk lounge suit he wore clung lovingly to his hard frame, the white shirt a sharp contrast to his lightly tanned face. She was humiliatingly aware of what a mess she must look in contrast, and the thought added fuel to her anger.

'Because, my sweet wife, I will not have you ignoring me.'

As if any woman could, she thought bitterly.

'I allowed you to play the martyr last night, to let you get it out of your system, and also——' he grinned wryly '—because I was too tired to argue any more. But today is the first day of our life together.'

'And the last,' she said bluntly. As the pale light of dawn had streaked the sky she had made her decision to leave Rayner. She had money of her own, she could find somewhere to stay, and there was no need for her grandpapa to know for at least a few months that her marriage was a farce. She had even considered an apartment in England somewhere—that way she could write home pretending all was well until a decent time had elapsed.

His face darkened with anger. 'You little fool. We stay together,' Rayner stated emphatically. 'The sooner you come to terms with the fact, the better.'

'Even though I regret ever knowing you, let alone marrying you,' she prompted vehemently.

His anger was replaced by a cold cynicism. 'You may regret the past, Marie, I'm sure we both do in our own ways. But now we are older, a mature married couple. At least, one of us is,' he qualified mockingly. 'You can't pretend you don't know what you're doing any more. You married me yesterday, and last night in my bed you were more than satisifed.' As he spoke his thumb gently stroked the inside of her wrist, while his fingers retained their fierce grip.

She blushed scarlet, and his blunt reminder of their lovemaking and the dual effect of pressure and gentleness on her flesh had a disastrous impression on her pulse-rate. 'So satisfied that I preferred to sleep on the sofa,' she derided, determined not to be seduced by his very

masculine charm into accepting this farce of a marriage.
She tried to pull her hand free, but he retained his grip
on her wrist.

'Is that by way of a challenge, Marie?' he asked silkily.
'If so, I should warn you my weapons are vastly superior
to yours, and I have no conscience about using them.'

'You have no conscience, full stop,' she snorted sarcastically, once more trying to pull free of his hold.

To her surprise, he let her go, but only to drag her
roughly into his arms, and before she could resist his
mouth covered hers in a kiss of bruising possession. The
heat of his hard body burnt through the flimsy protection of her robe, lighting a thousand nerve-ends in
her sensitive flesh.

She fought against the blatant attack on her senses,
and her small hands, curled into fists, struck out at anything they could reach, but he quickly overwhelmed her
resistance, and with her helpless to stop her body's
betrayal, her fingers uncurled and her hands slid willingly around his neck.

He went on kissing her, parting her trembling lips, but
gentler now, seeking her response, until she began
ardently returning his kisses. His lips left hers to trail
tiny kisses down her neck, and he nuzzled her throat,
his mouth closing over the pulse madly beating there,
and biting softly.

'It is a compulsive addiction, isn't it?' he demanded
coldly, holding her slightly away from him, but making
no attempt to free her.

She stared at his hard, handsome face, her own flushed
with a desire she could not hide. He was in complete
control of his emotions while she—she burnt with shame.
'Yes.' There was no point in denying the obvious, but
she had no intention of becoming his sexual slave—that
way lay destruction.

She had seen it with her own mother—slavishly devoted to Tom, she had put up with his free-love policy, which in Tom's case had been a licence to make love to whoever he fancied. For the first time, Marie realised why her mother had sought refuge in drugs—the pain of loving and betrayal had been almost impossible to bear.

'Your honesty does you credit,' he stated, a little more warmth in his tone. 'Now if you can be as realistic about the other areas of our marriage, I see no problem,' he concluded with a smile.

Somehow the thought of her mother gave her strength. She straightened her shoulders, determined to knock the complacent grin off his face. 'Really, Rayner, sex alone is not enough to keep me married to you. Why, I'm sure any one of a thousand men could satisfy me in that department, but I certainly would not marry for it,' she derided with a cynicism that rivalled his own. The grin vanished from his face as she watched.

'I see,' he drawled icily. 'You want to do it the hard way.' His hands fell from her shoulders, setting her free, but the hard implacability of his gaze kept her rooted to the spot. 'All right, Marie. Just exactly what do you have in mind?' He did not give her a chance to answer. 'Run back to your grandfather? I think not. He would not forgive you so easily—he didn't forgive your mother for years. Or perhaps you think an apartment somewhere, and after a decent interval a tearful reunion with Henri,' he said scathingly.

She flinched at the ease with which he had read her mind. 'It's none of your business what I decide to do,' she said with some courage.

'Ah, but it is, Marie. You walked out on me once, and there is no way I will let you make a fool of me twice. You will honour your marriage vows.'

'And if I don't?' she cut in impetuously. 'Will you force me?' she sneered, deliberately wanting to hurt him by a not too subtle reminder of his record.

'But we both know I won't have to,' he retorted, seemingly indifferent to her crude insinuation. 'Should you make any attempt at all to leave me, I promise you I will go straight to Henri with the truth about your early life, and I may just add a few embellishments of my own.'

'Grandpapa has a bad heart—you couldn't do that. It might kill him.' The thought of Rayner talking to Henri filled her with horror. Her shoulders slumped, all the fight knocked out of her. She would never forgive herself if anything happened to Henri.

'I could and I will. As I said before, I have no conscience where you're concerned.'

She stared up into his ice-cold eyes and she knew he was speaking the truth. 'You're a bastard...' she swore, her self-control finally broken.

'Then that makes two of us, darling,' Rayner responded cruelly. He absorbed her defeated face with arrogant amusement. 'Don't dish it out, if you can't take it, Marie,' he offered indifferently.

Why was she baiting him? She was no match for him, and she knew it. She recalled the morning after he had arrived at the château, and her conceited assumption that at last she could meet Rayner on an equal basis. Was there no end to her stupidity? she asked herself helplessly.

'You look a mess. Why don't you run along and clean up? I'll order breakfast.'

'You aren't very tactful, are you?' she sighed in defeat.

'Cruel to be kind, Marie. The past is over, forget it,' he commanded, slanting her a sardonic look. 'Today is the start of our marriage; I have the morning free, and

I fancy indulging my wife. Shopping, a wedding present perhaps.'

'I don't want anything from you,' she said curtly.

'You prefer to stay here...?' he prompted silkily.

Marie's heart missed a beat at the sensuous invitation explicit in his glittering grey eyes, and without a word she spun on her heel and almost ran to the bathroom.

She found herself staring at her own image in the mirror over the ornate bath. God, she thought, was that dishevelled, frightened-looking individual really her? No wonder Rayner said she looked a mess. So much for her smooth sophisticated image!

She piled her hair up on top of her head and fastened it with a few pins, then she paused for a moment to stare at the unfamiliar gold band on her finger. Yesterday it had meant so much, and today it meant less than nothing. Shrugging off her robe, she wished she could shrug off her thoughts so easily.

The warmth of the shower had a soothing effect on her taut nerves, and did much to relieve her aching muscles. She told herself it was the result of sleeping on the sofa that had left her body oddly sore, but deep down she knew it was a much more intimate reason.

Quickly slipping into clean underwear, she viewed the contents of the wardrobe with a jaundiced eye. She had no desire to wear the new clothes she had purchased for her trousseau. Instead, she selected the most conservative suit she could find, a plain grey wool she had packed at the last minute, thinking it might come in useful for everyday wear. With it she teamed a paler grey silk blouse, and, slipping her feet into plain black court shoes, she surveyed her image in the dressing-table mirror. She certainly didn't look bridal, in fact she looked like a hag, and with a sigh she sat down and opened her make-up case.

She used quite a bit more than usual, but then it took a lot more to cover the shadows under her golden eyes. She studied her reflection critically, added a touch of blusher to her cheeks and outlined her full, slightly swollen lips in a pink gloss. Her long red hair she scraped severely back off her face and clipped into a neat French pleat.

Finally satisfied, she stood up and, picking up the small black Chanel handbag by its gold chain, she marched into the room to join Rayner, angry and burning with resentment.

He emerged from the depths of one of the high-backed chairs, a cup of coffee in his hand. 'Better. Now, come and sit down and enjoy your breakfast.' And without waiting for her compliance Rayner turned and sat back in the easy chair.

Marie moved reluctantly across the room to take the chair opposite. On the occasional table dividing them was an array of food: hot flaky croissants, a dish of ham and eggs, bread, fruit and cheeses.

The thought of food made her feel sick, and she slowly sipped two cups of black coffee, while Rayner munched his way through just about everything. Obviously the events of the night had not disturbed him one jot, if his appetite was anything to go by, she thought resentfully.

Marie sat in the back seat of the taxi, and watched the streets of Paris flash by without seeing them. Rayner had instructed the driver to drop them at the Champs-Elysées—why, she had no idea. She could not see him as a typical tourist somehow. A self-derisory smile curved her full lips. A few weeks ago she had... How could she have been so blind? she asked herself for the thousandth time, so caught up in her own thoughts that she hardly noticed that the car had stopped.

She brushed aside the hand Rayner held out to her and alighted from the taxi unaided. The driver had dropped them at the Arc de Triomphe and for a moment she forgot her troubles as she gazed at the magnificent monument sparkling in the bright autumnal sunlight. It had only recently been repaired and cleaned for the two hundredth celebration of the Revolution and it looked superb. This should have been the happiest morning of her life, and instead...

'Where to now?' she demanded curtly, fighting down the bitter emotions that threatened to overwhelm her.

Rayner took her by the arm, and turning her to face him said softly, 'Lighten up, Marie. We're on our honeymoon, and all the books say Paris is *the* place for lovers.' He smiled down at her and for a moment she was almost fooled by the warmth in his grey eyes, until he added, 'And I did not imagine your passionate response last night. We are most definitely lovers.' The corners of his mouth curled in a cynical, knowing smile as his gaze raked her from head to toe. 'Though looking at the way you've dressed this morning you have done your best to hide any trace of the fact.'

Her severe hairstyle and plain suit had not gone unnoticed, and she was fiercely glad; it was a slight lift to her shattered pride. 'If you don't like my clothes, tough! I dress to please myself.'

'I don't mind in the least,' he drawled and, leading her along the broad pavement of the Champs-Elysées, he bent his head towards her. 'But then I have the advantage of knowing what you look like totally naked,' he murmured softly in her ear.

Marie could feel the colour rising in her face, and if they had been anywhere less public she would have slapped him—as it was she had to content herself with shooting him a filthy look. His grip on her elbow tightened, anticipating her desire to be free of his hold, and with a resigned sigh she walked by his side down the broad boulevard. Years of cultivating a cool sophisticated image prevented her from fighting with him in front of some of the smartest cafés in Paris.

It was only ten in the morning but already quite a few of the pavement tables were occupied, a smattering of tourists and the local Parisians reading the morning newspapers, or just watching the world go by.

'Where are we going?' she asked. Any conversation was better than dwelling on the past.

'I have it on good authority that if we walk almost to the bottom of the Champs-Elysées and turn right on to the Avenue Montaigne, there we will find some of the best designer shops in Paris. Personally I don't care how you dress, but in two weeks' time we are giving a large party for my friends and acquaintances. The invitations have already been sent.'

'How kind of you to tell me,' Marie cut in sarcastically.

Rayner ignored her outburst. 'I intend to see you have a suitably impressive gown for the evening, and anything else that takes your fancy. You will find me a not ungenerous man, Marie—so long as you fulfil your duties as my wife.' He slanted her a mocking glance. 'It has been my experience that women cannot resist spending a man's money, and I'm sure you are no different.'

'I don't want anything from you,' she informed him bluntly, appalled at his cynical attitude towards her sex, but at the same time her heart cried for the one thing he would never be able to give her. Love...

The Avenue Montaigne housed some of the great names in fashion—Christian Dior, Nina Ricci, and Chanel, usually Marie's choice—but Rayner had different ideas.

'You need something young, exotic, to match your striking colouring,' he told her firmly and dragged her into Valentino.

Marie had to suffer the indignity of parading past her husband in a multitude of gowns and separates. The clothes were beautiful, but much more flamboyant than she would ever have picked for herself.

The evening gown Rayner insisted she have was positively indecent to her eyes. In shades of autumn red, brown and gold silk, the strapless boned top hugged her full breasts, revealing far too much cleavage for her taste. The bodice fitted like a second skin to hip level and then flounced out in layers of silk to a handkerchief-hem skirt. It had a gipsy air to it, and she hated it, too much of a reminder of her early days, but after a low-voiced argument with her husband she had to give in.

'All right, buy the damn thing, but I've had enough— I want to go back to the hotel. Now.'

Marie waited impatiently while Rayner paid the bill and arranged for the clothes to be delivered to their hotel. He had not stopped at the one gown, but appeared to be giving the assistant a list of all the garments he approved of. Yesterday she would have been delighted by his action, but now it galled her to be indebted to him in any way. With a snort of disgust, she walked out of the establishment. Let him catch her up, she thought rebelliously.

Rayner caught her hand before she had gone three yards, and spun her around to face him.

'What is the matter with you now, Marie? I thought you would like shopping,' he said softly. 'Most women do.'

'But I'm not most women,' she bit out.

'You should have eaten some breakfast, it might have improved your disposition,' he drawled mockingly.

'After your behaviour last night, food would have choked me.'

'Too much exercise. Your sugar level is obviously low.' His eyes were amused, knowing...

'The only thing low around here is you,' she shot back.

She had gone too far—his face flushed dark with anger, the scar on his jaw stood out pale in stark relief.

'That is enough,' he said with deadly coldness. 'I let you get away with walking out just now, but I will not tolerate your childish insults. You may act like an outraged virgin with her romantic notion of love shattered, but we both know you're not. Your sexual needs match my own perfectly, and I only took what you were more than willing to give. And I've paid the top rate, a wedding-ring, and don't you forget it.'

Marie stared at him, her anger vanished, to be replaced with burning humiliation as his glance roamed insolently over her. There was a hunger in his eyes that lit an answering spark inside her. 'How could I?' she murmured to herself. Every time she looked at him there was a flare-up of sexual attraction, and she was for a moment bitterly conscious of her despairing love for him.

The taxi ride back to the hotel was completed in total silence. Marie chanced a sideways glance at Rayner. He was staring out of the window, a darkly brooding look on his hard face, seemingly completely impervious to her presence, while she felt as though every nerve in her body were being pulled tight with intolerable tension.

She dropped her head, but that gave her an even more disturbing view of his muscular thighs clearly outlined beneath the taut fabric of his trousers. When she found herself gazing at the hard bulge of his masculinity, she gulped and looked out of the window. God! What was happening to her? She had never been so intensely aware of him. Last night had not appeased her desire for him, but the reverse.

As a young man Rayner had taken her virginity with a sweet fumbling tenderness and she had responded with girlish enthusiasm, but last night she had been like one possessed, succumbing to his all-powerful intense masculinity with a fierce adult passion. She had loved him so much, wanted him so much...and it had all been lust...

Her lips twisted in a humourless smile; she laughed at her own naïveté. Tonight she would share his bed, she had no choice. If he touched her, she knew her body would betray her, but never again would her response be as uninhibited. He would not wring any declarations of need or love from her ever again.

She picked up her handbag and flung it over her shoulder, and stiff-backed she allowed Rayner to take her hand and help her out of the taxi. She sighed inwardly—if only she had not been so stupidly trusting. For her grandfather's sake she was going to have to continue with a mockery of a marriage. Where she would get the strength from, she did not know...

Since childhood she had encased herself in a protective shell, allowing no one to penetrate to her innermost feelings, with the exception of this man who walked by her side.

Marie glanced briefly at his forbidding features, and quickly away. Not once, but twice she had opened her heart to him, and all she'd got for it was excruciating pain. Well, no more, she promised herself. She had her writing career, it was enough...and she reverted back to her defensive shell.

Marie tossed her handbag down on the sofa, and sank into an easy chair. Rayner stood towering over her, his expression unreadable.

'I have to leave almost immediately for my business lunch. Would you like me to order something to be sent up for you?'

'No, thank you. I am quite capable of looking after myself, even if I have given you a contrary impression over the past few weeks. I'm not stupid,' she said coldly.

'In that case I can trust you not to try anything stupid...like running away while I'm out, hmmm?'

'As if I would,' she drawled sarcastically.

His perfectly arched brows rose in derision. 'Oh, you would, Marie, if you thought for one moment you could get away with it.' Bending, he rested his hands on the chair-arms, effectively trapping her, his grey eyes narrowed on her upturned face. 'Don't try it, Marie—think of Henri.'

She shivered, the sinister threat in his softly spoken words unmistakable. 'I wouldn't dream of it,' she said curtly, watching him warily—he was much too close for comfort.

He smiled. 'Good, I knew you would be sensible,' he murmured, and taking her chin between his finger and thumb he tilted her face to his.

Marie felt her pulses leap, and she was trapped by the dark intensity of his gaze as his silver head bent, his mouth fastening on hers in a sensual, teasing kiss. Her heart missed a beat, then raced, as his mouth coaxed her lips apart. She should be fighting him... She caught her breath as he broke the kiss and straightened to his full height.

'*Au revoir*, for the moment,' he drawled insolently. 'I expect to be back about four. Make sure you're here.' And he turned and walked out of the room.

She woke the next morning, not surprised to find herself alone in the king-sized bed. The previous evening hadn't been as bad as she had feared. Rayner had returned from his meeting in an oddly sombre mood. She had used the hours while waiting for his return to consider her position and build up her defences. She'd been proud of herself when she found she could face him with a poise and sophistication that matched his own.

He had suggested dining in the hotel restaurant and she'd coolly agreed. The meal had been perfect, the conversation desultory, and it had suited Marie perfectly. By the time they returned to their suite, a wide chasm had developed between them which she'd had no desire to try and cross.

Rayner had spent the rest of the evening studying some papers from his earlier meeting, and she had had a bath and gone to bed. When he'd entered the room some time later she'd pretended to be asleep, but she need not have bothered.

'There's no need to fake sleep, Marie. I don't take what isn't freely offered, and anyway I have a long drive ahead of me tomorrow to England. I have decided there is no point in prolonging our stay here,' he had informed her blandly, and then climbed into bed and turned his back to her.

In the cold light of morning Marie told herself she was relieved he had not tried to make love to her. If he no longer desired her, all the better. That was what she wanted, wasn't it?

By the time they arrived at Calais, she was a nervous wreck. Rayner had driven like a bat out of hell across the country, not saying a word. Marie sat in the passenger seat of the gleaming silver car long after he had finally stopped at the ferry terminal, trying to recover her nerve.

Rayner opened the car door and slid back into the driving seat. 'I've got the tickets, we can drive straight on. The boat leaves in five minutes.'

'So that was your reason for imitating Nelson Piquet,' she quipped, exchanging the first civilised words they had spoken all morning.

He laughed, a genuine smile curving his sensuous mouth. 'I did drive rather well,' he opined with smug satisfaction.

She took a deep breath—sometimes he could be so like the young man she remembered, it hurt. He was dressed casually in a soft blue cashmere sweater, and a pair of tight faded jeans that clung to his long legs like a second skin. She gulped—her thoughts were wandering along a dangerous path, and when they were eventually parked in the bowels of the vessel she hastily scrambled out of the car and made for the stairs leading to the upper decks.

She had grown up in the past two days, Marie thought as she stared out to sea. That small part of her that still trusted, still believed in faith and innocence against all the odds, through her traumatic childhood and teens, had finally fossilised into stone.

Reluctantly she turned her back on the coast of France, and walked stiffly to her husband's side...

Rayner pulled the car into the side of the road at the brow of a hill, and looked out of the window, a slow smile curving his firm mouth.

'There it is,' he said, pride evident in his tone. 'Your new home, Mrs Millard. I always think this is a splendid view of the house. Don't you agree?'

'Very impressive,' she muttered, and it was. In other circumstances she would have been overjoyed at the first glimpse of her new home. The house lay across an open expanse of parkland with an occasional great oak tree and copper beech to break up the rolling green of the valley. A long drive curved to a large, square stone-built house. The sun glanced off leaded and mullioned windows, a cluster of smaller buildings formed a small courtyard on one side of the house, and behind the trees framed the building, covering all the opposite hillside.

'Are we going to stay here all day admiring the view?' she asked waspishly.

'No, of course not. But I thought you might have liked to review old memories,' he said softly, turning to look down at her intently. 'It must seem familiar to you.' And he smiled...

'Why? I don't recall your ever handing out invitations to a poor little hippy,' she responded sarcastically. If he thought he was going to win her over to be a sweet little biddable wife with a smile and soft words, he had another think coming.

'I would have if you had given me the chance. Instead, after allowing me to love you——'

'Please can we——?' she cut in, disturbed by the way the conversation was going, and even more so by the searching look in his cool grey eyes.

'No, Marie, there is something that has always puzzled me about that night, and I want some answers. You allowed me to love you, I was young and hopelessly inexperienced, but I do remember you were with me all the way, avidly so,' he recalled mockingly. 'So why did you try to lay me out with a stick two minutes later?'

What the hell, she thought, he might as well have the truth, he could not hurt her any more than he already had. 'Because I didn't appreciate being a joke for you and your father,' she said bluntly.

The mockery vanished from his eyes, and his smooth brow creased in a puzzled frown. 'A joke? You must be mistaken, I never joked with my father about you. What on earth gave you that idea?' he asked with what almost sounded like genuine concern.

'Don't pretend, Rayner. You know exactly what I mean. Afterwards you burst out laughing and said, "A hippy! Wait till I tell my father." If that isn't making a joke out of a girl, I don't know what is. You knew how I felt about my lifestyle. I had confided in you. You knew I hated even the word hippy, but still you laughed at me,' she said bitterly, all her old anger returning. 'You're lucky I didn't smash your head in,' she added scathingly. 'It was no more than you deserved.' Still do, she told herself furiously, hadn't he fooled her again, and this time it was a hundred times worse?

'My God! Because of one stupid word, "hippy", I spent three months in gaol,' he exclaimed harshly. 'There was I trying to propose marriage for the first time in my life.' His grey eyes flashed sparks of pure rage. 'I said,' and he quoted in a tone that would have cut diamonds, '"Wait till I tell my father—the girl I'm going to marry is one of the travellers he's always so concerned to help."'

Marie stared at him, all the colour draining from her face at his words. She couldn't believe it.

'I was a besotted fool, but you with your red hair and temper to match were worse, flying into hysterics over a word,' he bit out scathingly. His hands tightened on the steering-wheel, his knuckles gleaming white with the effort to control his rage.

'What a waste!' he snarled, flashing Marie a look of such contempt that she shrank in her seat, and then with a grinding of gears he started the car and drove on.

Marie didn't say a word—she couldn't. If he was telling the truth... No. She dared not believe him, because if she did all the guilt would be hers and it would crush her. She could not bear it. She could not have been so wrong.

He had made up the proposal to clear himself in her eyes, so he would not be arriving home with an obviously reluctant bride. That must be it, she tried to reassure herself, but a devilish little voice deep inside reminded her that Rayner had still been talking when she'd struck out at him all those years ago...

CHAPTER SEVEN

THE interior of the house was as impressive as the exterior, Marie thought, following Rayner into a large square hall. She noted briefly the polished wood floor, a Chinese silk rug a splash of colour against the gleaming heron-bone blocks, and oak-panelled walls mellowed to gold with age, before he introduced her to a white-haired old lady, with a terse, 'This is Maisie, my housekeeper. She'll show you around and I'll catch you later.' And with a brief nod he disappeared through one of the numerous sturdy oak doors that opened off the hall.

'That man works far too hard,' Maisie said with an indulgent smile at his departing back, and turning to Marie she added, 'I'm so happy he met you again. If anyone can stop him working himself to death it's you, madam.'

Marie, still dazed at Rayner's earlier assertion that he had proposed marriage years ago, stiffened in shock at Maisie's words. It had never occurred to her that anyone would know about their past relationship, and she hated the thought. Perhaps something in her face communicated her feelings to the little housekeeper, because the old lady rushed to reassure her.

'I'm no gossip, don't you go worrying none. The poor man was so happy when he found you again he had to tell someone, and who else but me? I've been like a mother to the boy since his mother died when he was barely three.'

For the next half-hour Marie was treated to Rayner's life history as she was led through half a dozen reception-rooms. The old woman was obviously devoted to Rayner and had been from the day he was born, through changing his nappies to comforting him over the loss of his father. She assured Marie that Rayner was madly in love with her, and the Millard men only loved once and forever. 'In the genes, you know.'

'Yes, I'm sure.' Marie finally managed to get a word in. The last thing she wanted to hear was Maisie singing the praises of Rayner, and as for his loving her... What a joke! She was sorely tempted to tell the other woman what a conniving rat he really was, but instead she contented herself with a firm request to see the upper floors. 'I would like to see the bedroom and have a wash, if you don't mind.'

'Sorry, madam. My Ned is always saying I talk too much. But I'm that pleased to have the house lived in again, I was...'

Marie gave up—nothing was going to stop the old woman having her say. So she inserted a 'yes' at appropriate places until eventually they reached the master bedroom.

It was a symphony in peaches and cream, with complementary curtains and carpets. The heavy mahogany furniture prevented it from appearing too feminine.

'It's beautiful,' Marie murmured.

'Yes, well, the master picked it, said it had to be finished by this weekend. The whole house. I moved out, couldn't stand the smell of paint all over. But he wanted to please you... Now I must go and see to the dinner. You have a rest. Come down for a cup of tea when you feel like it. I would bring it up, but my legs aren't as good as they were.'

Marie shook her head in reluctant admiration for the other woman as Maisie walked out of the door. There was no question of her loyalty to Rayner, but Marie could not help wondering about her ability to work. She looked eighty if she was a day, and walking was a problem if her shuffling gait was anything to go by.

Her shoulders slumped in weary resignation, as her gaze slid to the pile of suitcases standing by the door. She should unpack, but she was reluctant to do so.

Marie let her eyes wander. It was a beautiful afternoon, and the sun streamed through the long windows, bathing the room in a rosy glow. She walked across to lean disconsolately against the window-sill. The view was breathtaking, rolling green fields, a variety of trees—oak, laurel, beech. A giant cedar tree claimed centre place on the front lawn, its massive branches extending in a huge circle of darkest green, a stark contrast to the autumn colours of its nearest neighbours. The landscape was reminiscent of a Capability Brown design. Perhaps it was an original... She'd have to ask Rayner.

The thought stopped her window-gazing. She was surprised she could see anything but the ordeal ahead of her. A sophisticated marriage, with no love. A polite charade for public consumption. Was she strong enough to play the part fate had cast for her? She had to be—she had no choice...

With a grim smile she turned her back on the magnificent view, and proceeded to unpack her suitcases. The heavy stuff—her typewriter, drawing-board and books—would be arriving Monday or Tuesday. She would have to speak to Rayner about a room of her own for an office. But she did not dare look too deeply at her willingness to share the master bedroom. She told herself she did not want to offend the housekeeper by asking for another room, and quickly hung her clothes alongside Rayner's in the row of wardrobes that covered one wall.

Marie stood balanced on the edge of a suitcase as she tried to slip another one into the top cupboard of the wardrobe. She was totally absorbed in what she was doing when a familiar deep voice drawled, 'You have great legs, Mrs Millard, and I would prefer they weren't broken.'

Her heart missed a beat, and she wobbled precariously on her perch as she turned her head to find herself looking down into Rayner's hard handsome face.

'Allow me,' he prompted, and, raising his hands to clasp her waist, he swung her to the floor, deftly taking the suitcase and tossing it in the cupboard. In seconds all the cases were disposed of.

'What are you doing?' she said coolly, glad he seemed to have dismissed the earlier angry exchange in the car. It was something she did not want to think about.

'Saving you from disaster,' he replied mockingly.

'I could have managed,' she muttered.

'Probably, but there was no need. You have me now...'

Rayner was standing so close to her, his masculine scent teased her senses. Dear lord, she groaned inwardly, if only that were true... How could she live in the same house as Rayner, loving him, hating him as she did? Marie looked up at him and murmured a grudging, 'Thank you.'

'So polite, Marie, you have changed—the other night you were all fire and passion.' He brooded over her stiff figure, and catching her chin between his thumb and forefinger he tilted her head back. 'I'm glad to see you're being sensible about sharing my bed. It doesn't do to repress one's sexual urges. It can lead to all sorts of complications.' His eyes darkened sensuously, and she knew he was going to kiss her.

She stiffened her slender spine and met his gaze. 'Something you have never suffered from, I'm sure,' she snapped, breaking the sudden tension in the atmosphere. 'As for the rest, your housekeeper never stopped extolling your virtues long enough for me to request another room, but I will. Now if you could please let go of my chin,' she said haughtily, 'I'm going to find the cup of tea Maisie promised earlier.'

He let her go, and, squaring her shoulders, she started towards the door.

'Marie.'

She turned back, as he called her name. Controlled...

'About Maisie,' Rayner warned, his eyes narrowing with glacial intent. 'She's gone to a lot of trouble to have the house ready for your arrival. You will not change rooms. I don't want her upset——'

'Have no fear, I'm not into mugging old women,' she jeered sarcastically, tacitly accepting his directive, but not prepared to acknowledge the fact out loud.

'I never thought you were,' he admitted with an edge of mockery, walking slowly towards her.

Marie raised guarded topaz eyes to his, taking in the hard cast of his rugged features. 'So?' she queried simply.

'If it makes it any easier for you, I will only be here at weekends. Monday to Friday I stay at my apartment in London. Once you come to your senses and get over your childish view of marriage you and I will get along very well. As for Maisie, she is a romantic at heart, and believes our marriage was made in heaven. I don't want her disillusioned. She's very dear to me.'

'I won't be the one to disillusion her,' Marie responded. The affection in Rayner's voice when he spoke of the old lady was unmistakable. Would he ever speak to her in that tone? She doubted it.

'Good. But there is——'

'What?' she cut in bluntly, desperate to get away from the much too intimate atmosphere of the bedroom.

Rayner's firm lips curved in a slow smile, his grey eyes lit with amusement. What was so funny? she wondered. But then, why shouldn't he smile, he had got all his own way, she concluded bitterly.

'Maisie has made a special celebratory dinner for this evening. Usually when I am here at weekends I dress casually, but tonight formal attire is a necessity. Otherwise Maisie will be insulted and give me hell.'

'Now that I would like to see,' she vouched drily. Later she was to realise just why Rayner had been amused.

She saw nothing of her husband for the next few hours, and after sharing a pot of tea with the housekeeper she returned upstairs. She took a long leisurely bath, first making sure the door was locked, and then, dressed in a full-length evening gown of black jersey silk, she added the finishing touches to her make-up.

She entered the dining-room with head held high, then hesitated, and her breath caught in her throat as she studied the man standing by a drinks trolley carefully pouring into two fluted glasses what looked like champagne.

Rayner in a black dinner-suit with a snowy white shirt and maroon bow-tie looked absolutely devastating, and she blessed the years of learning self-restraint that allowed her to accept the glass of wine he held out to her with a hand as steady as a rock.

'You look beautiful as always, my dear,' he casually complimented her, adding, 'Shall we sit down? I have a feeling this might be a long meal.' His lips twisted into a sardonic grin.

Marie took the chair he had pulled out for her and glanced around the room. It was impressive. A warm coal fire burned in a huge fireplace, and on the antique mahogany mantelshelf were scattered an assortment of fine Dresden figurines, an oddly feminine touch in what was a comfortable but formal room. The dining table was all of twelve feet long and Rayner sat at the head, with Marie on his right-hand side.

'Isn't this rather splendid for just the two of us?' she queried in an effort to break the silence. The subdued lighting, the flickering fire, the whole ambience of the room hinted at seduction.

'You have to make allowances for a foolish old woman who believes love makes the world go round,' Rayner responded with a cynical smile. 'She still mourns the loss of her husband fifty years on.'

'But I thought Ned——'

'Good God, woman, that's her son. Maisie must be eighty-odd, and Ned is in his early sixties.' Rayner laughed, and at that moment the lady in question shuffled into the room a huge soup tureen in her hands.

Marie felt like jumping up and offering to carry it for her, but she knew the woman would be insulted, and, taking a sip of her wine to steady her nerves, she waited patiently for Maisie to serve the soup.

At the first mouthful she almost gagged. The soup was lukewarm and had obviously come from a packet—the powder was not completely absorbed. She glanced covertly at Rayner, wondering if he had noticed. It did not seem so. His gaze was fixed expressionlessly on the plate before him, and he methodically raised the silver spoon to his firm mouth and disposed of the soup.

'You're not eating, Marie—Maisie will take it as an insult to her culinary skills if you don't clear your plate.'

Why did she get the feeling he was laughing at her? she wondered, as with grim determination she forced herself to empty the bowl before her.

The next course arrived some half an hour later, by which time an uncomfortable silence hung over the room. Marie had done her best, but Rayner had been no help, seemingly content to sit watching her, the barest trace of a smile playing around his sensuous mouth, as though in some way her attempt to preserve the niceties of dinner conversation amused him.

To her questions about the house and surrounding country he had responded with the briefest of answers, and when finally, out of desperation, she had asked who had painted the picture on the opposite wall, somehow it looked vaguely familiar, he had stunned her to silence by admitting it was one of her father's.

Why would he have a painting by Tom in his home? She knew they were very expensive, a good investment. Not that she got any of the money—some first cousin was his legal heir, and she had had no desire to query the fact. But Rayner was the last man on earth she would have expected to keep a Tom Brown painting—he hated the man. Hadn't he married her for revenge? Oh, he denied it, but she knew, there could be no other reason...and the swift stab of pain she felt she put down to hunger...

Marie was grateful for the diversion when Maisie returned pushing a loaded trolley, but her gratitude was short-lived when she saw the food set before her.

She stared in horrified amazement at potatoes boiled to mush. What might some hours earlier have conceivably been a steak was now a piece of black leather. To complete the disaster, brussels sprouts and cauliflower fought with each other as to which was the most waterlogged, and when Maisie held out the gravy boat Marie grabbed it eagerly. Perhaps if she covered the food in sauce... She stifled a groan as brown liquid flowed like treacle from the sauce boat, liberally spiced with black lumps.

'Thank you,' she said, and surreptitiously crossed herself before adding, 'That looks lovely, Maisie.' May

God forgive her the lie. She watched Maisie's retreating back with disbelieving eyes.

Marie had never been particularly fussy about food, but she could cook reasonably well. How on earth had the woman kept her job as a housekeeper all these years, when it was obvious she couldn't cook worth a damn? She turned her head towards Rayner. Was he actually going to eat this rubbish? she asked herself. Surely not...

'Dig in, my dear, you don't want the food to get cold.' He returned her stunned gaze with a bland look.

'Get cold,' she repeated parrot-fashion. Years of always doing the right thing saw her lifting a forkful of potatoes to her mouth, and, closing her eyes, she swallowed. She shot a sidelong glance at Rayner to see if he was faring any better, and was surprised to find his head bent over the table, his broad shoulders shaking uncontrollably.

'What is it?' she demanded worriedly—perhaps he had choked on the meat. 'Are you all right?' She reached out her hand and grasped his forearm. He did not answer. 'Speak to me, Rayner!' she cried in real fear. She heard a splutter, a choke. 'Rayner!' My God! He could be choking to death, she thought, rising from her chair to stand over him. He sounded desperate. Then to her amazement he threw back his head, and roared with laughter.

He laughed till the tears came to his eyes, 'Oh, Marie, if you could have seen your face,' he howled, slapping the table with his hand. 'I have never seen anything so funny in years.' Still laughing, he grasped her hand. 'The soup nearly choked you, but when you looked at the dinner and crossed yourself I almost broke up then... I would never have believed it possible. You would hang on to that cool poise of yours even if it killed you.' He wiped the back of his hand across his eyes to brush away the tears of laughter.

'Why, y-y-you swine, you knew...' she stuttered with fury. All the time she thought he was ill, dying, he was laughing his stupid head off at her. She tried to tug her hand free—she would choke the devil herself. She swore violently in both French and English. But he tightened his grasp on her fingers, refusing to let her go.

'Ah, come on, Marie, we always used to share the same sense of humour.' His grey eyes danced with laughter as they scanned her flushed and furious face.

Her lips began to twitch—he was right. Her glance slid over his broad shoulders, immaculately encased in a superbly tailored dinner-jacket, and she looked down at her own evening dress. There they were, dressed up to the nines, with a meal in front of them that a dog would turn up its nose at.

Her full lips parted in a broad grin. She collapsed back down into her seat, her hand still held in Rayner's, and burst out laughing. So that was what had amused him earlier, she thought. He must have known all along the meal would be a catastrophe. His suggestion that they had better sit down as the meal might take a long time was obviously the voice of experience speaking. Poor Maisie's rate of walking must be somewhere around a mile an hour, if that.

She raised her head, her golden gaze clashing with sparkling silver, and for the first time in ages they shared a moment of sheer delight.

'But if you know she can't cook, Rayner, why on earth do you employ her?' Marie asked when she had got her breath back sufficiently to think sensibly. 'And what are we going to do about this food?' She would hate to hurt the old dear.

'I have it all under control. Why do you think we have an open fire?' And picking up her plate and his own he stood up and swiftly swept the offending food into the fire. Returning the plates to the table, he turned and added a couple of large logs to the spluttering flames.

'Such foresight, and very efficient,' Marie chuckled, as he resumed his seat. 'But there is one small problem. I'm starving, and if that was a true reflection of your housekeeper's culinary skills, I will die of malnutrition if I stay here for any length of time,' she informed him with a teasing grin.

'Even as I speak a huge plate of chicken sandwiches is waiting in the study. As for Maisie, she was never employed as a cook, but originally as my father's nanny, and then mine. She belongs here, and when my father died and the cook left there was no need to employ another one for the few days I stay here.'

Marie listened with interest as he continued. She was getting an insight into his character that totally contradicted the hard image he usually portrayed to the world.

'Obviously, now you are the mistress of the house you will want to make your own arrangements, but Maisie won't be a problem—she has her own apartment on the top floor, she spends most of her time there, or else she stays with Ned and his wife at their cottage about a mile away. At weekends she insists on looking after me, but actually the reverse is true, I watch out for her, and during the week I employ a couple of ladies from the village, more to keep an eye on Maisie than to look after the house.'

'It does you——' She had been going to say 'credit', when Rayner shushed her, and, bending his head to hers, whispered behind his hand.

'Here she comes—not a word, and actually her puddings are quite edible.'

To Marie's surprise the dessert was good, a delicate chocolate sponge with a thick creamy custard. She ate it with relish, but she couldn't help wondering why, if Maisie could make such a perfect custard sauce, her gravy was a lumpy disaster? She said as much to Rayner and he laughingly replied,

'I would never dare question my old nanny. Don't ask.'

The lack of much food, and the empty bottle of champagne left on the table, were responsible for Marie's mellow mood as she meekly followed Rayner into the study.

Maisie had left with her son Ned for the rest of the weekend, but not before insisting on clearing up, and embarrassing Marie by wishing her a happy honeymoon.

Now, comfortably seated in a large leather armchair, her shoes kicked off and her feet curled up under her, Marie tucked into the sandwiches Rayner had so thoughtfully provided.

'More champagne.'

She raised her head; Rayner stood towering over her, a bottle in one hand and a full glass of wine in the other. In silence she reached out and took the glass, his fingers brushed hers and a tingling sensation shivered up her arm. Suddenly all her senses were alerted. They were alone in the house, and very soon she would have to climb the stairs to the master bedroom.

She lifted her glass to her lips and drained it. For a while this evening she had forgotten the true state of their marriage, fooled by his laughter and concern for someone other than himself, but now, as she glanced up at him through the shield of her thick lashes, all her fears returned.

His eyes glittered mockingly down into hers as he caught her surreptitious glance. She was alarmingly aware of his tantalising masculine attraction. Her heart skipped a beat, a slow flush burnt up under her skin—she tried to tell herself it was the wine, but she knew it was a lie. She was mesmerised by the darkening gleam in his eyes, and when he reached out his hand to trail one long finger down her arm she nearly jumped out of her skin.

'I'm going to bed.' She shot off the chair and, pushing past him, placed her glass on a table by the door, almost running out of the room.

She washed quickly and slipped into her lacy night-dress, cursing the fact that she had not packed any less provocative clothes, but then at the time she had thought she was marrying the man of her dreams.

She sat down at the dressing-table and unpinned her hair, and picking up a brush she swiftly swept the long mass of red-gold curls back off her face with hard, sure strokes. No one hundred tonight—she wanted to get to bed and asleep before Rayner arrived, but she was too late...

She had not heard him enter and she gave a startled gasp as his hand closed over hers, taking the brush from her nerveless fingers.

'Allow me, Marie. You have the most beautiful hair I have ever seen.'

'Ginger,' she deprecated, in an effort to cover her nervousness.

Pyjama trousers hanging low on his hips were his only covering, the dark golden hairs on his muscular chest appeared tipped with gold in the subdued lighting. He was magnificent.

'No, never ginger, more like living flame,' he husked softly, and, deliberately bending over her, his lips found the soft skin of her throat in a fleeting caress.

'Don't.' She squirmed, but he ignored her plea, and dropping the brush on the table he swung her around and up into his arms, murmuring words, dark, husky, exciting words, into the gentle curve of her throat. She had never realised before that just the sensuous sound of a man's voice could be so arousing. Her breasts hardened at the contact with his bare chest, the thin film of lace no protection against the erotic sensations he was arousing in her.

'Ah, Marie,' he growled roughly, raising his head, and his grey eyes burnt down into her before his mouth closed over hers in a long, devouring kiss. She felt his hands cup her buttocks, and pull her firmly into the masculine cradle of his hips. The hard length of him left her in no doubt of his intention, and she trembled on the brink of submission.

It took every ounce of her will-power to push herself out of his arms, but she had to if she wanted to retain her self-respect.

She hastily stepped back and stared up into his handsome face, which was flushed with passion, his grey eyes gleaming black with barely controlled desire.

'What the hell——?' he exclaimed in puzzlement.

She almost laughed at the expression on his face— obviously he was not used to being refused.

'No, Rayner, you said I would have to ask, and I won't, not ever...'

'Don't be stupid, Marie,' he groaned, and hauled her back into his arms. 'You want this as much as I do, why deny ourselves the pleasure?' he demanded, and his mouth sought hers, his expertise in no doubt as he went on kissing her, delving deep, with a sensual mastery that made her dizzy and aching for more.

'No!' She tried to resist him as his hands swiftly removed her nightdress. It was sex, just sex. She meant nothing to him except an available body to while away a pleasant hour. How could he be so hard? So un-feeling? her mind cried.

'Yes.' His voice thickened. 'Before long you will be begging me.' And, shifting slightly, his eyes raked her flushed features and tangled curls, before dropping slowly to rest on the pulse throbbing visibly in her throat. 'You want me,' he said flatly.

She gazed at him helplessly—the rough pressure of his chest against her breasts was a pleasure-pain she fought desperately to control, but humiliation burned her face as he held her slightly away from him and studied the evidence of her arousal. His silver head lowered, his tongue trailed down her throat, over the soft rise of her breast, and then his mouth closed hot and moist over the rigid peak.

She stifled a groan of pure pleasure, but when his hands roamed to curve her hips, bringing her into intimate contact with his lower body, she realised that now he was also completely naked. The hard evidence of his desire throbbed against her belly and all her re-sistance vanished.

'You can't remain cold in my arms for long, Marie.' The rasping words grazed her flesh as Rayner lifted his head, his grey eyes glittering with passion and pure mas-culine triumph.

She flinched but could not deny the truth of his words. He swung her up in his arms and crossed to the bed, laying her gently down on it and quickly dropping down alongside her.

'It is nothing to be ashamed of, Marie,' he said throatily as if reading her mind. 'You are the most sensual woman I have ever touched, the most hot-blooded.' His hands stroked and caressed her as he spoke, and warm, quivering sensations raced through her body, setting every nerve-end alight with need.

'I love to feel the way your body responds to mine,' he husked throatily, his lips once more finding her breast, slowly tracing a circle around the hard nub, teasing, tantalising.

This time she could not control the groan of pleasure that bubbled in her throat, and winding her small hands in his silver-blond hair she urged his head up to hers. Their lips met in hungry passion, and as Rayner rolled on top of her their bodies melded together as one.

'You want me, Marie,' he rasped. 'Say it, say it, Marie.' And she did...

Marie slept soundly for the first time since her wedding-day. She awoke to find herself alone in the bed. Where Rayner was she did not know, and told herself she did not want to. Quickly she bathed before dressing in a cream wool pleated skirt, a tan silk shirt, and low-heeled tan pumps.

She was sliding the final clip into her thick hair to hold the neat chignon in place when Rayner walked into the room, carrying a tray with cafetière of coffee on it. She looked at the tray, then up at his face. Their eyes met, hers wary, questioning, and his slightly mocking.

'Don't imagine I'm going to make a habit of this.' He indicated the tray with a nod of his head as he placed it on the dressing-table. 'But, not surprisingly, we rather overslept this morning,' he taunted silkily.

The colour rushed to her face, as the events of the night flashed vividly in her head. He had made love to her till dawn, and she had been powerless to resist him. 'Thank you,' she said stiltedly, lowering her eyes, unable to hold his mocking glance. She felt the brush of his lips on her hair, before he turned and walked to the door.

'Have your coffee and be quick—it's quite a drive to church.' He flung the words over his shoulder as he closed the door behind him.

Marie had adopted the Catholic faith whole-heartedly within a few months of arriving in France. But it had never occurred to her that Rayner would be a regular church-goer.

She stared with sightless eyes at the room as the full implication hit her. She did not believe in divorce, but somehow she had imagined Rayner would divorce her without a qualm when it suited him. Now she wondered... Not that she would ever marry again. She was married to the only man she would ever love. But Rayner—did he intend this charade to be a life sentence?

She filled a cup with coffee and quickly swallowed it down. Thinking about the future was a fruitless exercise. She was having enough trouble getting through one day at a time. Hastily she donned the dogtooth tweed jacket that complemented her skirt, and, stuffing a few essential items in the matching tan shoulder-bag, with a last look in the mirror she left the room.

He was right about the drive, she thought, puzzled why he would travel for almost an hour to Bournemouth to go to church. Surely there must be one nearer. Then guilt flooded through her—perhaps she was indirectly responsible. He had told her his friends had looked sideways at him after the case... Maybe that was why he no longer attended his local parish church.

Standing next to Rayner at the altar rail for Communion, she had to swallow hard to prevent her emotions overcoming her. Was it only four days ago, she asked herself, when she had stood at a very similar altar and vowed to love, honour and obey this man? For better or worse? She choked back a bitter sob of self-pity. Well, she had certainly found the worst part. She cast a sidelong glance at Rayner, tall and remote, his face a hard mask, the curving scar an ever-present reminder of just what she had done to him. God help her! She could see no hope for the better...

They left the church side by side, but not touching, and for the first time in her life Marie did not feel the uplift attending mass had always given her in the past.

Rayner, without consulting Marie, stopped the car at a delightful pub on the edge of the New Forest. 'Lunch here is excellent, and after last night I'm sure we could both use a decent meal.'

The food was delicious: traditional roast beef and Yorkshire pudding, accompanied by a selection of fresh vegetables and horseradish sauce. For pudding Marie chose from the sweet trolley a fantastic concoction of peaches and almond sponge and lashings of cream, while Rayner chose cheese and biscuits.

She looked up from her empty plate to find Rayner watching her, a smile curving his sensuous mouth.

'You ate that like a child,' he opined. 'It reminded me of the first time I saw you, a couple of years before I ever spoke to you. You were a child then, all legs and wild red hair, wandering around the countryside, but always on your own. With the travellers, but never of them. Later, in France——'

'I had plenty of friends at home,' she interrupted. She did not want Rayner analysing her; the thought that he had watched her as a child was disturbing and she was vulnerable enough already.

'You know plenty of people, that's true, yet at our wedding the only bridesmaid was your cousin. No bosom pals in evidence. I'm beginning to realise you don't let many people near you.'

A cynical, angry Rayner she could handle, but a questioning, analytical Rayner was far too dangerous. So she

responded derisively. 'Isn't that rather the pot calling
the kettle?' A more guarded man than Rayner would be
hard to find.

'Do you want to get to know me better, Marie?' he
queried quietly, almost as if her answer mattered to him.

'Certainly not.'

Rayner laughed, a harsh sound. 'That doesn't surprise me. Come on, let's go.' And, abruptly rising from
the table, he paid the bill and they left.

The journey back to the house was completed in a
tense silence.

On entering the house, Rayner suddenly grabbed her
arm and rushed her into the lounge, shoved her down
on the sofa and switched on the television.

'Good, we're in time.' He sat down beside her.

Before she could argue at his high-handedness her
attention was caught by the picture on the screen. In the
turmoil of the last few days she had forgotten all about
the big race.

They watched in silence as the cameras unfolded the
beauty of Longchamp, and the start of the Grand Prix
de L'Arc de Triomphe. She caught a fleeting glimpse of
her uncle Jacques and her grandfather before the horses
were led to the starting stalls, and the race was off.

She watched with bated breath until the horses reached
the final furlong, and excitement overcame her. She
jumped to her feet screaming, 'Come on, Supreme!'
Then Rayner leapt up and swung her round and round
in his arms. Jacques's horse had won.

'I'm sorry you weren't there, Marie, but I thought it
might be difficult seeing your family quite so quickly.
Yesterday you hardly looked a blushing bride,' he
mocked lightly.

His apology surprised her. She had forgotten all about
the big race in the trauma of her wedding night, but now

her eyes sparkling with pride and excitement rose to his. 'He did it. Jacques did it—Supreme won!' she cried in elation, and missed the flash of regret in the grey eyes smiling down into her own.

'This calls for champagne.' And, sliding her slowly down the length of his body, Rayner set her on her feet. 'I won't be long,' he said roughly, and left.

With time to think, Marie collapsed into the nearest chair, her eyes filled with joy and sadness. Joy for her uncle. It was a dream come true for Jacques, she thought emotionally, but her own dreams had faded and died ...

She gratefully accepted a glass of champagne from Rayner, the tears running down her face as she watched the screen and her uncle and aunt accepting the most coveted trophy in the French racing world.

Later in bed with Rayner he made love to her with a gentleness she had never experienced before.

The next morning he left for London, but first, with Ned's assistance, one of the attic bedrooms was quickly converted into the office she had requested.

CHAPTER EIGHT

LEAVING Maisie to answer any queries, Marie dodged out of the back door and, turning the collar of her soft tweed jacket up around her ears against the chill October wind, she set off walking, through the garden and into the trees. Tonight was the grand party to introduce her to Rayner's friends, and the house was overflowing with caterers, cleaners, florists, all arranged by Rayner. Everything was going smoothly, her presence wasn't required...

Once hidden from the house by the woods, she slowed her steps and looked around. It was a beautiful, clear, crisp afternoon, and she certainly needed the fresh air. Everything was organised for the party, except for the fact that her husband had not yet arrived back from London.

Rayner was a strange man and a complete enigma to her. She thought back over the past two weeks, and had to admit they had not been as bad as she had feared.

In fact, she thought musingly, her lifestyle had changed very little. She worked at her writing most days. Lost in the realms of her fantasy people, she found she could blot out for long periods of time the disaster of her marriage. The little fairy-like insects who lived in the huge French fields of sunflowers were in a way her salvation. As long as she had her work she could almost bear the rest.

The hardest part to come to terms with was the night. She tried to tell herself she was glad when he was away, but she didn't know which was worse, lying in the big bed on her own, the light of dawn in the sky before she could sleep, or sharing it with Rayner, and falling asleep exhausted, satiated in his arms, but hating herself for her inability to resist him, when she knew he did not love her.

She kicked viciously at some fallen leaves, wishing they were Rayner's shins. He surprised her in so many ways, she could not understand him at all. Sometimes lying in his arms, their bodies wet with the sweat of love, clinging to each other, she could almost believe he cared for her, then she would remember their wedding night, and she knew she was fooling herself. He was a hard, ruthless man without a heart.

Yet he called her every night when he was away. Their conversations were mostly about the estate, but it was still contact. She wondered why he bothered, but in the next breath she was glad he did.

She had met the estate manager, Geoff, a keen young man not long out of agricultural college, with an attractive young wife, Jenny, and an adorable year-old baby girl. They were coming to the party tonight.

Marie shivered and pulled her jacket closer around her. She was dreading the evening ahead. All the local dignitaries were expected to attend, and a couple of people from London were staying the night. She hated the idea. She had said as much to Rayner on Monday morning as they had drunk their breakfast coffee, together, before he departed for London. But he had lightly dismissed her fears.

'My dear Marie, it will be your moment of glory. I can hear all the good people now, wondering how a disreputable character such as myself managed to capture the stunningly beautiful, and half-French—Ooh, la la—Marie Doumerque,' he drawled teasingly.

'It's not funny, and there's no need to be sarcastic,' she snapped.

'I wasn't being sarcastic. You are stunningly beautiful,' Rayner responded, catching her hand in his across the table. 'Now suppose you tell me what is really bothering you,' he demanded hardly.

He could read her far too easily, she thought resentfully, though it wasn't surprising—he had been watching her like a hawk all weekend. She had tried to keep out of his way, but everywhere she turned he had appeared, studying her as though he had never seen her before. She knew just how a deer must feel, stalked by the hunters, and it was unsettling to say the least.

She wished he had stuck to his callous attitude of the first couple of days of their marriage. Whatever game he had decided to play, she wanted no part of it. She didn't trust him. How could she? A charming, affable Rayner was a threat to her already overtaxed nerves.

'Marie, I asked you a question.'

'What? Oh, yes.' For a moment she'd been lost in thought—worry would be a better word, she thought wryly.

'So, are you going to tell me?' His fingers tightened on hers, she lifted her head and her gaze was trapped and held by the grim determination of Rayner's expression.

'What if anyone recognises me?' She blurted out the fear that had been nagging at the back of her mind for days.

'Is that all?' And dropping her hand he stood up and walked around to put a strong arm about her shoulders. 'Don't worry your head about it, Marie—so what if someone does? I'll protect you, I promise.'

His familiar touch, the warmth of his hard body, had been comforting and somehow she had believed him.

Thinking about it now gave her an odd little tingle of pleasure. She was perhaps being foolish, but when he had finally left that morning he had stunned her by calmly announcing that he intended to work from the house in future, with only an occasional trip to his head office in London.

Then he'd hauled her up into his arms, and before she could resist had kissed her very thoroughly. Long after she had heard the sound of his car drive away she had stood in the kitchen, wondering what had softened his attitude towards her.

She disturbed a flock of crows and their raucous cries brought her back to the present with a jolt. They flew up in the air, dozens of them, wheeling and circling above her head. For a second she envied them their freedom. How she wished she could fly away and forget her troubles—and the nagging feeling of guilt, she wryly admitted. She could not quite exonerate her own behaviour seven years ago, no matter how she tried.

She sat down on the grass, resting her back against a gnarled oak tree, and looked around. She had walked further than she had intended, and for a moment she did not recognise her surroundings, then it hit her like a fist in the stomach. It was the same small clearing she had shared with Rayner years ago.

She started to rise, and then gradually sank back to the soft grass—running away, she told herself, would not help. Perhaps here, in this place where it had all started, she might be able to get some order to her thoughts, some perspective to her strange marriage.

She could understand Rayner believing she was a dreamer out of touch with reality, but it was not strictly true. She had a vivid imagination—she could not have made a success of her writing otherwise. But she had a determined methodical streak, a trait she had developed as a child, maybe as a rebellion against her lifestyle. It was ironic really; other children rebelled against their parents and dropped out, while she had only ever wanted to drop in...

She breathed deeply of the cool air and slowly expelled the breath on a sigh. She had a premonition that tonight would be a turning-point of some kind in her marriage, and it was up to her to decide just what she was going to do. For the last couple of weeks she had felt confused, hurt, angry, but also a deepening love she could no longer deny.

It seemed to Marie that she had two choices. She could go on as she had, avoiding Rayner as much as possible, for the most part stiffly polite, except in bed where he would not allow her to be anything other than passionately involved. Or she could accept his practical view of marriage, and try to make the best of it.

She knew what her grandpapa would say. She had spoken to him frequently on the phone, and somehow he had recognised that she was not quite a deliriously happy bride, as he had informed her quietly that all good marriages needed working at. She had quickly reassured him everything was fine. Worrying Henri was the last thing she wanted.

She shivered; bending her legs, she wrapped her arms around her knees and rested her chin on them. The question was, could she bring the same determination to bear on her marriage as she had on the rest of her life? She was a strong woman, even if in the last few weeks she had acted like a wimp. She had fought for her education, she had fought to build a successful career. Was she prepared to fight for her marriage?

There was only one answer. Yes... Rayner did not love her, but as far as she knew he did not love anyone else. Propinquity was a great asset, and he wanted her, he never tried to deny it. There would be children, maybe sooner than she wanted, she thought ruefully. It was too soon to tell, but she was already a week late with her period. He had promised to protect her, and he accorded her all the civilities of a wife. According to Maisie, he loved her—maybe he had once. He had told her that as a young man he had been a besotted fool, and had asked her to marry him. If she accepted that, and tried hard enough, maybe, just maybe, she could make him love her again.

She chuckled, feeling more light-hearted than she had in weeks. There were an awful lot of 'maybe's in there. Her gaze roamed around the little glade and suddenly she sobered. She was forgetting one vital factor. If he had married her for revenge, nothing she did would make any difference. True, he had denied it, but she had not believed him.

If she was to make a success of their marriage, she was going to have to give him the benefit of the doubt. What had he said? It suited his sense of justice. Perhaps she could live with that. She consoled herself with the thought that it had been coincidence he had seen her in Deauville. He had not gone looking for revenge...

The crunch of footsteps on some dying leaves startled her. She jumped to her feet, and turned to see Rayner stalking into the clearing. There was no mistaking his tall lean figure, and the incongruity of his city suit in the middle of the woods brought a smile to her lips.

'Marie.' His voice reached her before he did. 'Where the hell have you been?'

She shivered, the smile wiped from her face by the anger evident in his tone. 'Rayner, when did you get back?' she responded, her gaze roaming helplessly over him.

Marie's heartbeat raced. His pin-striped jacket moulded his broad shoulders, he had pulled his tie free and his white shirt lay open at the neck, revealing the light dusting of hair on his chest, his dark trousers clung lovingly to his powerful thighs—he was all predatory, aggressive male.

He stopped beside her. 'Don't you know you shouldn't answer a question with a question?' He towered over her, and in her flat walking shoes she had to tilt her head back to see his face.

Some imp of mischief made her respond, 'Why not?'

His mouth quirked with amusement, and she could almost see the anger drain out of him. 'I asked for that,' he replied cursorily.

He was staring at her intently, his eyes fixed on her face, and Marie had the strange feeling that his mind was not on what he was saying. He reached out to her, his strong hands clasping her shoulders, while his gaze lingered on her mouth, then slid slowly lower over her slender form before once more returning to her face.

'Yes, you did,' she retorted. 'And I haven't been anywhere,' she finally answered his original question. 'It's like a madhouse down there, I wanted some fresh air,' she explained.

'I know,' he muttered, his gaze unwavering on her face. For a long moment the only sound was the wind rustling through the leaves of the surrounding trees.

Marie was intensely aware of Rayner's hands on her shoulders, the musky male scent of him, his vital male form so close to her own. Her pulses raced and, with her earlier decision in mind, she took a hesitant step closer. She was beginning to feel uneasy. There was something odd in his eyes—it was as if he were drinking her in. 'Rayner,' she murmured.

His fingers tightened on her arms—she could sense the tension in him.

'I arrived back from London, and I thought you had gone,' he said softly, so softly she had to strain to hear him. 'I couldn't find you in the house, or anyone who knew where you were.'

She raised her eyes and topaz mingled with silver-grey. 'I told Maisie.' She swayed closer still, trapped by the darkening gleam in his eyes. His arms folded around her, and he lowered his head, his mouth finding hers in a long, achingly tender kiss.

'I hoped I would find you here. This is our place, Marie, you recognised it.' He slurred the words against her throat, then raising his head he demanded hardly, 'Didn't you?' daring her to deny it.

Marie flushed and nodded her head; his kiss, his tenderness, had stolen her breath away. She was looking up at him, unconscious of the effect of her huge topaz eyes under thick dark lashes, and the soft swollen fullness of her mouth, combined with her aura of cool restraint, was a tantalising challenge to any man, and Rayner was no exception.

She felt him shiver as his arms tightened around her. 'Are you cold?' she asked with concern.

Throwing back his head he laughed, a harsh, sharp sound in the quiet glade. 'No, my sweet, never cold, not with you, it would be an impossibility,' he derided in a dry, self-mocking tone.

It was an admission of sorts, and the unexpectedness of it stunned her. Their eyes met, his desire was instantly communicated, but there was something more. It wasn't just need or passion, it was as if they had slipped into a time-warp, and were once again the hopelessly young couple, poised on the brink of discovery.

Rayner dropped his arms, freeing her from his hold, and stepped back, but his eyes never left hers. He removed his jacket and laid it on the ground. Then, with hands that trembled, he dealt with her jacket in the same way. Heat surged from the centre of her body to every part of her, and she recognised the power he had over her as he drew her close again.

His slight nervousness enthralled her, his raw sexuality enslaved her, and when he picked her up in his arms and laid her on the ground she saw something in his eyes that made her heart turn over in her breast.

His fingers fumbled with the buttons of her shirt, and she covered them with her own, helping him to undress her. Within seconds they were both naked, hands and lips seeking, urgent. They came together in a frenzy of unashamed need. The place, the broad daylight, forgotten in the urgency of their passion.

Marie lay, her head pillowed on Rayner's chest, and listened to his thudding heartbeat beneath her ear. Her body felt heavy, but her heart was lighter than it had been in weeks. For the first time since their marriage Rayner had made love to her and completely lost control. They both had. Her eyes closed, and, her hands delicately stroking the soft hair on his broad chest, she savoured the knowledge, loving him, and glorying in his impetuosity and her own.

'I intended to ask if you missed me,' Rayner's voice rasped, 'but I think I know the answer.' And folding his arms tighter around her soft body he added, 'I missed you, Marie.'

His admission in a voice husky and gentle was the sweetest words Marie had ever heard. She shivered, but not with cold, exulting in their moment of closeness—maybe he was beginning to care.

'You're trembling. My God, I must be crazy—it's almost freezing.' And rising to his feet he held out his hand to her and pulled her up beside him. 'The middle of October is no time to be making love outside,' Rayner chuckled, carefully helping her on with her clothes.

His grey eyes smiling down into hers, his lean fingers brushed her cheek, and he looked at her quietly, then bent his head and kissed her so tenderly that it made her heart sing.

Trance-like, she stood and watched him, unashamedly delighting in the play of muscle in his broad back, and firm buttocks, as he retrieved his crumpled clothes and put them back on.

'You're ogling, Marie, and, much as I would like to oblige, we do have guests arriving very shortly.'

'The party!' she exclaimed, her dazed mind finally beginning to function. 'My hair!' She frantically ran her hands through it, dislodging a shower of leaves. 'What time is it?' she groaned in dismay, and to her chagrin Rayner flung his head back and burst out laughing. 'It's not funny,' she muttered, shoving her feet into the brown moccasins.

'It is to me, darling, the oh, so proper former Marie Doumerque, with leaves in her hair and grass stains in unmentionable places,' he roared.

'You're no picture of sartorial elegance,' she shot back, grinning at his once beautiful jacket rumpled and dirty. Their eyes locked, gold mingling with grey, a companionable warmth, and something else Marie was too afraid to name, flowing between them.

'You were right, Marie,' Rayner mused, his lips quirking with humour as he glanced around the familiar glade. 'One day we will laugh with our grandchildren over this place.'

Her heart lurched, and she fought for breath. Dared she believe him? Was it possible his thinking could alter so drastically in a few short weeks? She stared in amazement at his cheerful, smiling face. He looked genuine, and his smile encouraged her to share the joke. Tentatively her lips parted in a reciprocal grin. She would once more take him at his face value, and she prayed this time he had no ulterior motive...

He caught her hand in his and raised it to his lips in an oddly gallant gesture. 'I'm sorry, Marie. I wish we didn't have to give this damn party. We need to talk, but now is not the time. Later, hmm?'

The round fat face of Chief Inspector Jones turned bright red as he roared with laughter. Marie had not thought the joke that funny, but in her position as hostess she dutifully chuckled.

Over his shoulder Marie's eyes clashed with Rayner's, she felt a tiny jerk to her heart-strings, and involuntarily her lips parted in a slow, warm smile. Rayner looked magnificent in his dark dinner-suit, the party was going perfectly, and all her earlier fears had vanished.

They had returned to the house with only an hour to spare before the arrival of their guests. A tingling warmth spread through her body at the memory of the shared shower...

She glanced down at her left hand, where the diamond solitaire Rayner had given her glittered brilliantly on her slender finger—a belated wedding present, he had said. She could see again in her mind's eye his almost boyish grin as he had slipped it on her finger an hour earlier. She felt like pinching herself to make sure she wasn't living in a dream. The transformation in Rayner's behaviour was a miracle.

'Enjoying yourself, darling?' The softly spoken words surprised her. Lost in her thoughts, she had not noticed Rayner's approach. But quite spontaneously she leant back into the arm that curved around her bare shoulders.

'More than I thought possible,' she responded, luxuriating in the pressure of his hard body firm against her back.

'I'm not sure that dress was such a good idea, after all. You look ravishing, and every man in the place is wondering what's underneath,' Rayner's deep voice claimed possessively in her ear.

Marie chuckled and tilted her head back to look up at him. 'Does that include you?' she teased.

'For God's sake, don't lean back like that; my nerves can't stand the strain, and neither can that dress by the look of it.' His gaze slid to the creamy mounds of her breasts, displayed by the strapless bodice of her gown, and swiftly he turned her into his side, dropping his arm to her waist.

The Valentino dress had created quite an impact, Marie thought smugly; the colours really suited her. The boned bodice clung to her luscious breasts as though it was moulded to her, the skirt swirled around her long legs in a rainbow of gold, red and brown, and with her Titian hair loose and curling around her shoulders to hang halfway down her back, she portrayed a primitive sensual appeal that, if she had realised it, would have horrified her.

'You're a lucky man, Rayner. Your wife is charming, and she laughs at my jokes.' The inspector's compliment was music to Marie's ears.

'I hope you haven't been regaling her with some of your more risqué ones,' Rayner prompted with a grin.

'Doris would kill me if I did,' the inspector responded bluntly.

Marie laughed out loud at the incongruity of the chief's statement. She had met his wife—she was a tiny bird-like woman barely five feet tall.

'Don't be fooled by her size. Explosives come in little packages,' he joked, and at that moment his wife joined him.

'I heard that, Cedric. Talking about me behind my back, shame on you,' she teased. Then turning to Marie she said, 'My dear, I've just found out who you are, and I'm so happy for you. It's like a fairy-tale come true. Of course, I never believed the rumours about Rayner. It was a lover's quarrel. I can still remember when Cedric and I were first courting—fought all the time, we did. But look how we turned out, and I'm sure you and Rayner will be wonderfully happy. A friend of yours, Rayner, the tall blonde lady, was telling me all about it. Oh, here she is. Isn't it marvellous—I do so like happy endings. My heartiest congratulations, Marie.'

Marie never knew afterwards how she got through the rest of the night . . .

As the evening had progressed she had begun to relax and thoroughly enjoy herself. The only slight unease she had felt was when Rayner had introduced her to one of the last couples to arrive: a journalist friend of his called Jake, and his girlfriend Lisa.

Marie had got the distinct impression that the arrival of the stunning-looking blonde model had been a nasty surprise to her husband, but in the ensuing hours she had forgotten all about it. Now, as the tiny Doris prattled on, Marie felt the blood drain from her face and it was only by the most almighty effort of will she managed to retain a fixed, polite smile.

'Thank you, Doris.' She accepted the congratulations with all the composure she could muster, and watched in rising horror and humiliation as Lisa strolled up to Rayner and placed red-tipped fingers on his arm.

'And such a tidy ending, Rayner darling,' the tall blonde drawled cynically. 'They were weeping into their champagne at Annabelle's when the news arrived. The silver fox finally snared—how droll.' She turned feral blue eyes on Marie. 'But Marie, I wasn't surprised. Under the circumstances you were the only woman he needed to marry.'

Marie was struck dumb by the viciousness of the other woman's attack. Needed, of course. Now she finally understood why Rayner had married her. His equation of justice was completed by her presence at his side tonight. With blinding clarity she saw it all: she was here to clear Rayner's name before all his old friends. The silver fox—how appropriate, she thought bitterly. 'Sly' was only one of the adjectives she would have liked to shout at Rayner. She felt as though her heart had been cut to pieces, and the hardest cut of all was to know that Rayner had confided his plan to Lisa.

Acting out of her skull, she turned limpid eyes to Rayner. 'It was Rayner who snared me, and I'm truly grateful he did.' No way was she going to let them know how much she was hurting.

'Yes,' he agreed and expanded on his affirmative. 'It has taken me a lot longer than I originally envisaged to trap my lovely wife, but now I have I expect to spend the rest of my life in connubial bliss.' He squeezed her waist affectionately then relaxed his hold to turn to Lisa. 'As for you, Lisa, I might have known you couldn't resist a gossip,' he opined, laughing down into the blonde's upturned face.

Marie stiffened and stepped carefully back, distancing herself from the small group. With blank eyes she gazed around the room; the laughter, the conversation swirled around her but she registered little of it. She was blessedly numb, frozen in shock.

Her eyes sought Rayner's in one last desperate appeal, hoping against hope that she was wrong about him, but all his attention was centred on the inspector, his handsome face betraying no sign of embarrassment at Doris's crushing disclosure as he laughingly recalled his unfortunate stay in gaol, and the punch on the selfsame man's jaw that had helped to keep him there for months.

Swinging on her heel, she grabbed a glass of champagne from the tray of a passing waiter. Her mouth was as dry as the Sahara. She took a deep swallow of the sparkling liquid, and blessed the years she had spent learning to hide her true feelings.

The astounding news that she was the girl who had caused the old scandal in the Millard family swept the room like wildfire. She suffered through another round of congratulations, her lips peeled back against her teeth in a parody of a smile. She felt as though she were walking through a nightmare. Earlier she had delighted in his friends' good wishes, but now she wanted to run away into a corner and hide...

'What do you think, Marie darling? Marie, I think you've had enough champagne,' Rayner teased, sliding his arm loosely around her shoulder. 'You haven't heard a word John was saying.'

She looked up. John was a tall, distinguished-looking gentleman of some sixty years. 'Sorry, I'm afraid I was miles away,' she apologised politely.

Rayner shot her a quizzical glance. 'John was asking me if I would stand as the Democratic candidate in the county council elections. Can you see me as a politician?'

'Yes, I think you would make a marvellous politician,' she gushed. Black rage surged through her, sweeping away the all-enveloping numbness that had protected her for the last half-hour. The swine, the no-good, rotten, machiavellian swine, she thought furiously.

Marie felt physically sick with anger and humiliation. Thank God the first guests had begun to leave. If she could just hang on another ten minutes, she could escape with her pride intact, even if her reputation never would be again, she thought despairingly.

But there was more to come. Jake and Lisa were staying the night, and as she walked back into the drawing-room, while Rayner secured the door for the night, she found her torture had not ended. A very drunk Jake grabbed her arm.

'I'm sorry, Marie. I should never have brought Lisa here. But when you're in love you do stupid things. She begged me to bring her, and I was foolish enough to hope it was because she wanted to be in my company. I should have known. She was Rayner's lover until you turned up again. I'm a stupid drunken fool—forgive me, Marie.' He stumbled and fell on to the sofa, letting go of her arm in the process.

She leant against the drinks trolley and looked down at him, trying desperately to hold on to her anger—instead all she felt was a searing pain in her heart. She had never before believed hearts could break, but now she did—hers had just splintered into a million pieces.

She could sympathise with Jake. They had both been played for fools.

'Pour me a nightcap, Marie darling, I could use a stiff drink. I didn't drink much of the bubbly.'

Rayner's deep melodious voice echoed in her brain, but she ignored his request. She turned slowly, and her topaz eyes clashed with soft grey. 'Get it yourself,' she said curtly, and walked out.

Rayner's voice followed her into the hall. 'What the hell have you been saying to her, Jake?'

How like Rayner, she thought with a flash of insight. He always had to blame someone else. His ego was so inflated it never entered his head that he might sometimes be at fault...

Naked, she stood under the freezing shower. Some corner of her mind registered the opening and closing of the bedroom door, but it did not break through her trance-like state. The cold water cascaded over her hair, her face, her ice-cold flesh, and she welcomed it. Welcomed it as only someone who could not bear the internal agony any more.

'Marie—are you all right in there?'

The handle of the bathroom door rattled. She ignored it...

'Marie—answer me, open the door.' The voice was louder now.

Carefully, like an old woman, she turned off the tap and slowly stepped out of the shower. With slow methodical movements, she rubbed her icy body dry, and then slipped over her wet head a sleek satin night-dress. Picking up the matching robe, she pulled it on and fastened the tie-belt firmly around her slender waist. Now anger edged the fierce demand for her response. She briefly towelled her wringing wet hair, and combed it straight back off her white face, then stiffly she walked to the door and unlocked it.

'What the hell were you doing in there?' Rayner demanded, catching her hand in his and almost dragging her to the centre of the bedroom. 'My God, you're frozen!' he exclaimed.

'Don't touch me,' she said quietly, and pulled her hand free.

'Marie, darling, what is the matter? The party was a great success. It was a triumph for you. I've never felt

so proud in my life,' he said, and would have taken her
in his arms, except she stepped around him. He swung
on his heel. 'Marie!' Exasperation creeping into his tone,
his grey eyes sought hers.

Coolly she faced him. 'A triumph for you, Rayner;
for me the ultimate step into the real world. Tonight I
at last discovered the true reason for our marriage. You
have succeeded admirably, Rayner. Your reputation is
restored with all your old friends. How could it be
otherwise, when the girl you were rumoured to have
raped is now your wife. Clever, very clever,' she said
scathingly.

'You're being ridiculous, Marie. I had no such
intention. It was unfortunate the old gossip was resur-
rected, but it didn't do any lasting harm. Our marriage
will be a nine-day wonder and then forgotten. You're
far too sensitive about your past. Nobody gives a damn
nowadays,' he said carelessly, shrugging off his dinner-
jacket, his hand unfastening the tie at his neck and
casting it aside.

Marie could sense the powerful tension within him for
all his apparent casual discarding of his clothes. She
watched him shed his shirt, and step out of his trousers.
Wearing only a pair of black briefs, he reached out to
her.

'You're cold and tired, Marie. We can talk in the
morning. Come on to bed,' he said sombrely. 'Today is
a new beginning for us.'

For a second she weakened, the sight of his hard muscular frame so enticingly near, his strong hand stretched
out to her. A woman's light laugh split the silence—Lisa
in the corridor.

Marie looked at Rayner with desolation in her empty
eyes. 'No.' She knocked his hand away. 'Today you made
a complete and utter fool of me for the last time. Stupidly

I believed you were beginning to care for me.' She spread one hand out in front of her and tore the diamond ring off her finger. 'You didn't have to give me that to keep me sweet for your guests.' She flung the ring in his face. 'A few kind words in the wood had already done the trick.'

His mouth curled, something dark and dangerous leaping to life in his eyes. The ring lay where it fell, ignored. He studied her wet tousled appearance, the flaming hair tumbling down about her white face. 'This afternoon you wanted me. I don't believe you've changed so quickly,' he said in a deadly quiet voice.

'No, this afternoon was a mistake,' she spat as he folded his arms around her rigid body.

His mouth came down on hers with a bruising angry pressure, intending to compel her submission. His hard thighs were imprinted against her softer curves as he pulled her tight against the long length of him.

She froze in his arms, offering no resistance, her hands hanging limply by her sides. Sex, that was his answer for everything, that was how he had manipulated her before. The kiss softened, begging a response, but she felt nothing, nothing at all...

Slowly he raised his head, sensing her complete withdrawal. She stared up into his darkly flushed face and said slowly and deliberately, 'Never again, Rayner—if you want sex try Lisa, I'm sure she'll oblige.'

CHAPTER NINE

'YOU'RE jealous,' Rayner drawled slowly, a self-satisfied smile curving his lips.

The conceit of the man was incredible, Marie thought cynically. Her total lack of response had not dented his ego one bit, instead he was grinning like a cat that had swallowed a bowl of cream, convinced the green-eyed monster was all that bothered her, and flattered at the thought.

'You have no need to be, darling.' And, pulling her back into his arms, he laughed. 'Whatever that fool Jake told you about me and Lisa was over long before I met you again.'

But his laughter was the last straw to Marie. Tonight her whole world had crumbled to ashes, and he casually dismissed her hurt and pain as nothing more than feminine jealousy.

'Jealous!' she screeched, shaking with emotion, and all the years of cool control, all the years of rigid self-restraint went up in flames in the grip of the most venomous fury she'd ever felt. 'Never in a million years!' she threw at him, her topaz eyes blazing, her face taut with rage. 'You arrogant, conniving swine. It isn't enough that you took everything I had to give seven years ago and laughed in my face. No, you had to come back and separate me from my first real home, my family, with lies and deceit, and you're still laughing...'

Rayner was slowly turning pale, and his arms fell away from her. 'Marie, no——'

'No, hell!' she shot back. Her fists clenched by her sides. 'All the years I wasted avoiding other men, because of you. Nurturing a fantasy dream of romantic love. On our wedding-day I would have lain down and died for you, and you had the gall to sneer at my morals. You, who in your supreme arrogance could stand in the house of God, and lie through your teeth.' Her impassioned speech gave away more than she knew, and she did not see the look of stunned realisation on Rayner's face.

'Marie, darling, please...!' He moved towards her.

But she backed away, too engrossed in her own hurt and anger to hear his plea. 'Well, you've got it all now, and I hope you're satisfied. Tonight you stood by and saw my reputation torn to shreds. You laughed while I cringed with humiliation. Do you think I don't know what those people were thinking? I actually heard a frosty-faced matron declare that for a little nobody I'd done very well for myself. My God!' She shook her head at the injustice of it all.

'Tell me——' Rayner asked curtly.

'Oh, I'll tell you all right. You have succeeded beyond your wildest dreams. You demanded I face up to reality. Tonight I finally have—the scales have fallen from my eyes and I can see you for the ruthless bastard you are. A career in politics will suit you to perfection, but I wouldn't vote for you if you were the last man on earth. I hate and despise you, and if I never see you again, it will be too soon.'

A strong hand enclosed her wrist. Rayner jerked her against his hard body. 'That's enough, Marie.' He swore savagely. 'You're becoming hysterical. If you will listen, I can explain.'

She did not wait for his explanation—his confining hand on her wrist snapped the last thread of her fragile control, and swinging her free hand in a wild arc she slapped his face with all the force she could muster.

'Don't touch me!' she cried. 'Not ever again.'

'That's it,' he snarled and picking her up he flung her on to the bed, his big body following her down, trapping her beneath him.

Marie struck out at him, but quickly he caught her flailing hands and pinned them above her head on the pillow. She was powerless to move, and the anger drained out of her like a burst balloon, to be replaced by fear.

'You are going to listen,' he told her through gritted teeth. She felt the tension in him, and her heart lodged somewhere in her throat. He had himself under control, but the banked-down anger was evident in the icy glitter of his narrowed gaze. 'I did not plan tonight as a dénouement. I did not know Jake was bringing Lisa— a month ago he had a different companion. I have no idea how Lisa knew about you. I admit I had a brief affair with her but it was over long before I met you again, and I certainly didn't so much as mention your name to her.'

'Perhaps she's psychic,' Marie jeered, to mask her pain at the knowledge of his affair with Lisa. She tried to move within his imprisoning hold, but her attempts were useless against his superior weight and strength, and all she achieved was a greater intimacy as her flimsy nightgown rode up round her waist. Rayner's briefs were the only barrier between them.

'It's the truth, Marie,' he said thickly, suddenly releasing her wrists, and moving his hands to clasp either side of her head, forcing her to look at him, their faces only inches apart. 'I laughed and joked about it because there was no alternative. What would you have me do? Act the outraged host and call the party to a halt? Now that would have caused a scandal,' he opined roughly.

'I believe you.' She didn't care that it was a lie. All she wanted was to be left alone. She was mentally and physically exhausted by the events of the day, and the fierce glitter in his grey eyes told her his silent anger was suddenly transforming into sexual desire.

He moved restlessly against her, his breathing slightly erratic, but his gaze level and unwavering on her flushed face. 'Now, why do I get the feeling you're lying?'

'Probably because you're so good at it yourself,' she retorted bitterly, throwing caution to the wind. She didn't trust him and she would probably never trust another man again. 'Now get off me. I loathe you,' she whispered, her small hands shoving against his broad chest, the hate inside her blinding her to the consequences of her actions.

'No, damn it, you're my wife.'

'I hate——' She never finished the sentence, as his mouth crushed hers, once again, bruising in its intensity. It was a brutal invasion which numbed and shocked her.

In growing desperation Rayner savaged her mouth, his hands stroked her smooth flesh, his legs nudged her thighs apart and he slid between them. She felt the surge of desire that gripped his body, the dampness of perspiration breaking out on his skin.

'You want me, Marie,' he told her hoarsely. 'Say it. Damn you, say it.' He groaned the words against her throat.

'No, no, I don't,' she said flatly. His body moved against her, and for a fleeting instant she thought he was going to take her anyway. She felt his hand between their bodies, his fingers curling around the waistband of his briefs. But his muscles clenched rigidly, and with a supreme effort of self-control he rolled off her, and slid his feet to the floor.

He sat on the edge of the bed for a while, appearing stunned, the rasping sound of his breathing the only sound in the room. Then at last he stood up, and stiff-backed walked to the window opposite.

'Tonight I almost did something I swore I would never do: force myself on a woman.' Rayner's harsh voice broke the tense silence. But he did not turn around. Marie lay where he had left her, hardly daring to move. She watched his broad shoulders hunch and his head bow; if she hadn't known better she would have thought he was in pain.

He ran a hand through his hair. 'You hate and distrust me, and what nearly happened just now can only confirm your low opinion of me.' Slowly he turned, his face hard, his eyes shadowed. 'Doesn't it, Marie?'

'Yes.' She gave him the answer he was expecting. Why was he bothering with a post-mortem? Everything between them was finished.

'I can't say I blame you. I haven't been particularly kind to you since our wedding.' He walked back to stand beside the bed, looking down at her with a strange lingering glance.

Marie fumbled with the coverlet and pulled it up over her scantily clad body. 'No, you haven't,' she replied, and cringed away from him as he sat down on the bed, depressing the mattress with his weight.

'Oh, God! Don't do that, Marie. I'm not going to hurt you,' he ground out. 'I won't touch you.'

'I wouldn't let you,' she said coldly.

An unfathomable expression flitted across his face. 'On our wedding night you swore you loved me. You couldn't get enough of me.' He cupped his hands in front of him, linking his fingers, and stared down at them. 'I had you in the hollow of my hands, and threw it all away.' He raised his head and met her eyes. A cynical, humourless smile curved his firm lips. 'If I told you now I loved you, would it make any difference?'

'No.' For a second Marie regretted her quick negative, but the ice-grey of his eyes told her she had made the right reply. He did not love her, never had. More manipulation, but now she was immune...

Rayner grabbed his robe from the foot of the bed and slipped it on. 'I'll sleep in my study. Tomorrow, when the guests have gone, pick any room you want.'

Marie clattered pots and pans around the kitchen, seething with resentment. The sound of laughter floated through from the breakfast-room. It's all right for some, she thought angrily. How she would love to tell the superior Lisa to cook her own breakfast.

Better still, a wicked smile curved her lips, she could go and call Maisie and let her cook it. That would soon knock the smile off the faces of her guests. She sighed. It was no use—years of training prevented her doing anything other than act as the perfect hostess.

Half an hour later she wished she had let Maisie do her worst. Sitting at the breakfast table watching Lisa and Rayner was enough to make her sick. Jake, poor soul, took no part in the conversation, in fact he was having great difficulty in keeping his bloodshot eyes open. But Lisa more than made up for him.

Marie was left in no doubt that her husband and this woman had once been lovers, probably still were, she thought cynically. She had never considered what Rayner did when he was in London. 'Humph,' she snorted disgustedly. Well, now she knew...

'Did you say something, Marie?' Rayner asked casually.

He knew damn well she hadn't, but smiling sweetly she rose to her feet and replied, 'Yes, does anyone want more coffee?'

'No. I'm swimming in the stuff.' Jake came alive. 'And we have to leave now.' He glanced at his watch. 'I'm due at the paper by two.'

Marie could have kissed him. Thank God! A few more minutes and she could escape to her books and drop the mask of polite civility she had been forced to adopt all morning. But the charade was not quite over.

Lisa's parting shot was a *coup de maître*. Standing on the front step of the house, her hand resting on Rayner's arm, she turned to Marie with a saccharine smile.

'Thank you, Marie, for a wonderful stay, and so interesting. I'm sorry we have to rush away, but to be honest the country life is not for me.' And giving Marie's tweed skirt and soft wool sweater a disparaging glance she added, 'I can see how it suits you, though, and this is a magnificent old house.' She turned her beautifully made up face to Rayner. 'But personally, darling, I much prefer your penthouse in London. You should bring your wife up to see it some time.' And with an airy wave to Marie and a kiss for Rayner she swanned down the steps to where Jake waited patiently in the car.

'Wait!' Rayner's harsh demand echoed in the large hall.

Marie stopped at the foot of the staircase, and looked back over her shoulder. 'I'm going upstairs——'

'You can change your bedroom later.'

'To pack,' she continued as if he had never spoken. 'I'm leaving.' She had tossed and turned all night trying to decide what to do, but the last five minutes had clarified her position in her own mind. There was nothing for her here.

Rayner was standing a few paces away from her, his face pale and drawn.

'Missing Lisa already, are you?' she sneered. It was amazing how his easy smile had vanished as soon as the car had driven off, she thought bitterly. 'You should have ridden with her—I'm sure it wouldn't be the first time.'

A flash of unfathomable anger drove the paleness from his face, and in one long stride he was at her side, his hand grasping her arm, and he towered over her. 'Crude innuendo is not your style, Marie,' he opined bluntly.

'So I've changed.' She shrugged, her anger rising sharply at his detaining hand on her arm. His fingers bit into her flesh. 'I've joined the real world, as you suggested. You should be pleased.' His hand fell from her arm and she stared up at him, her chin jutting defiantly. She was her own woman and, from now on, she was going to stay that way. Her golden eyes blazed challengingly into his.

His hard face was all planes and angles, the skin pulled taut across his cheekbones; the scar on his jaw stood out white in stark relief against his tanned complexion. She had the oddest feeling he was fighting some silent battle she could not comprehend. Rayner breathed deeply, and looked away, avoiding her eyes.

'Yes, you have, and it's my fault, I freely admit it. But Marie, you can't leave. I can't allow it. If you——'

'You can't stop me, unless you use force, but then we both know you won't do that,' she snapped back sarcastically.

'Please, Marie. I won't argue with you. Five minutes in my study, that's all I ask.'

She did not want to listen to him, but she supposed five minutes could do no harm. 'All right, but make it fast, I want to pack.' She allowed him to lead her into the study.

She sat down in a soft leather chair, but did not relax, her back straight and her feet crossed primly at the ankles as she waited for him to speak. Rayner prowled around the room, picking up one object after the other and replacing them. If she didn't know him better she would have thought he was nervous. But the swine didn't have a nerve in his body, she thought venomously.

'I think we should call a truce, Marie.'

'What for?' His words made no sense. 'You've won the war—after last night your reputation is spotless and you're totally acceptable again. You've got everything you wanted,' she said flatly.

'Not quite everything, Marie, if you recall…' he hinted silkily. Her head shot up and met his mocking gaze, and deliberately he let his eyes roam over her slender form and back to her face. 'No, not everything I wanted, hmm?'

For once the familiar flush did not rise to her face. Instead Marie looked at him with no emotion to haze her judgement. He was leaning against the large oak desk, his silver-blond hair was slightly ruffled, his lips were curved in a deliberate sensuous smile, the soft blue of his cashmere sweater reflected in his eyes. One hand was shoved in his trouser pocket, pulling the fabric of his navy trousers taut across his thigh; only his other hand playing idly with a paperweight betrayed he was not as relaxed as his casual stance portrayed. Dispassionately she admitted to herself he was a perfect example of vibrant masculinity, but it was wasted on her.

Marie stood up—her disillusionment was complete; she despised him, and all he stood for. She smiled with relief. 'Keep your sexual teasing for your lady-friend,

Rayner,' she sneered, as he straightened abruptly, his lips tightening in a firm line. 'I've become immune to your particular brand of charm, and, at the risk of sounding repetitive, I'm going to pack.'

'Where exactly do you intend to go?' Rayner asked, taking a step towards her, his strong hand closing around her wrist like a manacle as she would have left the room.

Marie hesitated; she had not thought that far ahead, she only knew she had to get away from him.

'Well, Marie?' he prompted.

She looked up at him. His grey eyes held a curiously intent expression, urgent almost, and before she could form a reply he continued.

'Certainly not your grandfather. Henri is a deeply religious man. He has an old-fashioned view of marriage, and if you tell him the terrible truth—as you see it,' he inserted with a flash of sarcasm, 'Henri will send you straight back here. I have spoken to him often on the telephone in the past couple of weeks. I doubt if he will believe I am the ogre you seem to imagine.'

Marie's eyes widened in surprise—she had no idea Rayner had kept in touch with her family, and glumly she recognised that his summation of her grandfather's character was spot-on. It was galling to admit that he was right, and resentment made her reply forcefully.

'I have no intention of going back to France. The way I feel right now, I would rather roam the country as a traveller—something I swore never to do again—than stay a day longer as your wife.'

It wasn't true, but she didn't care. She wanted to lash out at him, hurt him any way she could.

She expected a furious reaction; instead to her surprise he simply arched one brow sardonically and said, 'Such a drastic measure will not be necessary, Marie. Suppose you stay here, but not as my wife. Obviously you no longer want me, and I can understand that. But surely you must see that, if you leave this house now, all those good people who were congratulating me last night will once more be doubting my integrity if you disappear again. This is a big house, so there is no reason for you and me to meet often. I will keep my business centred in London, and will rarely be here. You can surely keep up appearances for the odd social occasion, and for the rest you can do what you like.'

Years later she would still be wondering what her answer was, or if she even gave one, as at that moment Ned burst into the study.

It was Maisie—he had popped up to her apartment and found her lying on the floor. The doctor arrived, a broken hip was diagnosed and the ambulance sent for.

Maisie was lying so still that Marie doubted she was still breathing. Ned was sitting on the side of the bed, his mother's frail hand clasped in his. Rayner stood at the opposite side, his face a blank mask, only the grim glitter in his grey eyes betraying the worry and pain he could not quite disguise.

Marie's heart went out to the two strong silent men; she wanted to help, but they were barely aware she was in the room, their whole attention centred on the still form of the old lady lying between the stark white sheets of the hospital bed. Maisie, in every way that counted, was mother to both men.

A single tear rolled down Ned's cheek and was quickly brushed away by his jacket-sleeve. Rayner's hands were clenched tightly by his sides, the knuckles gleaming white with the strain.

According to the doctor, Maisie must have felt unwell and gone to her apartment. The signs were that she had had a slight heart attack and fallen, hence the problem with the hip. But the operation appeared to be a success, though recovery would be a slow process—Maisie's age was against her, he had warned. Now, six hours after arriving at the hospital, they stood around the bed willing the old woman to revive.

A nurse walked quietly into the private ward. 'I'm afraid you will have to leave now. But don't worry,' she straightened the pillow and curled her fingers around Maisie's wrist, 'she's doing fine, and you can come back in the morning.'

Rayner drove back to the house on the Saturday night with an absolute silence between them. Had it not been for Ned's occasional demand for reassurance about his mother's condition, Marie would have burst into tears. She was haunted with guilt and remorse.

If only she had checked on Maisie last night, she thought frantically—she should have known something was wrong. When Rayner had met her in the woods, he said no one had known where she was. Marie should have realised then that Maisie would never have willingly left a house full of strangers unsupervised. Later Marie had been too enthralled by Rayner and the party to even give the old woman a thought.

The car stopped and Ned said a mumbled goodnight and vanished in the gloom of his front yard.

'It's all my fault,' she blurted as Rayner drove on again. 'I should have checked on Maisie last night, and this morning if I had called her at breakfast. I thought about it. I actually considered letting her feed your friends—serves them right, I thought, and all the time Maisie must have been lying on her own in pain.' She blamed herself and her voice broke on a sob.

'You have nothing to reproach yourself with. Maisie was my responsibility and I failed her. Something I seem to be making a habit of lately,' Rayner responded, an odd roughness in his deep voice.

'No——' It was entirely her fault, she was the mistress of the house, and she had failed in her duty by not checking on the housekeeper. Rayner cut her off.

'Please, Marie. I can do without your arguing tonight.'

She swallowed a lump in her throat and didn't say another word.

The headlights lit up the front of the house, and a brilliant white Mercedes sports car that should not have been there.

'Oh, no, not visitors,' Marie groaned—she could not face anyone right now. With brutal honesty she silently admitted she could not bear to face herself.

'It's OK, Marie. There's no one here. I forgot to mention...' Rayner hesitated, wearily pinching the bridge of his nose between a finger and thumb then rubbing a hand across his broad forehead. He turned to look at her. 'It's for you. I told Henri to keep your little Renault, it wasn't worth bringing back to England.' And drawing a key from his pocket he dropped it in her lap, then swung around and out of the car.

She picked up the key and turned it over in her hand. He must have ordered the car days ago. She looked in confusion at the key and then at the gleaming new car. Why would he buy her something so expensive? And last night the ring...

She jumped out of the car and followed Rayner into the hall. Of course, remembering the ring clarified her thoughts immediately. The car was just another example of the image he expected his wife to portray, she answered her own question, burning with resentment.

'You had no right to tell Grandfather I didn't——'

Rayner turned, his hand on the knob of the study door. 'Shut up, Marie, just shut up.'

'How dare you speak to me——?'

'For God's sake, woman! You have a chip on your shoulder the size of the Rock of Gibraltar. Does it never occur to you I might just like buying you presents? Why can't you accept a car, or a ring, without looking for an ulterior motive?'

'I realise your motive all right,' she flared. 'The right image for your wife.'

'You're good in bed. They could be for sevices rendered,' he drawled mockingly.

Hot colour flooded her cheeks. 'That's a despicable thing to say,' she spluttered.

'Is it? No more despicable than this pointless argument. Why not try forgetting your repressive self-centred view of life and think about someone else for a change? Maisie could be dying...'

The scathing contempt in his voice made Marie cringe in shame. He was right—now was no time to start yet another fight.

'I'm sorry. I'm going to bed,' she murmured, and proceeded to walk past him.

'Marie.' His voice stopped her halfway up the stairs. 'I meant what I said this morning. Except that under the circumstances I won't be returning to London until I'm assured of Maisie's full recovery.'

'I understand,' she responded wearily, and adding a mumbled goodnight she carried on up the stairs.

Half an hour later she was lying in the queen-sized bed in the guest-room, fast asleep.

That night set the pattern for the next few weeks. Marie visited Maisie every day in the hospital, sometimes by herself, and sometimes with Rayner. The strain of behaving as a happy couple in front of the old woman was intolerable to Marie, and she tried to keep joint visits down to a minimum.

She saw surprisingly little of Rayner. Occasionally in the morning he would be in the kitchen when she went down, and they would share a silent breakfast. To her surprise he was quite a good cook, and he prepared the morning meal as often as she did. In the evening they shared dinner, which was completely her domain, after Rayner remarked that his cooking skills did not extend beyond ham and eggs.

Rayner had turned into an aloof, polite stranger. He went out of his way to make sure he did not touch her, except in front of Maisie. Every night immediately after they had eaten he retired to his study to work, with a curt goodnight, leaving her to go to her solitary bed.

She told herself it was what she wanted. She hated him, didn't she? But as October slid into November the icy anger that had frozen her emotions so completely began to diminish under the weight of compassion she felt for her husband.

Maisie was not recovering as quickly as she should and the constant worry, the thirty-mile travel to the hospital every day, was a strain on them all, but more so for Rayner, who still had his business to run.

Also, looking at their relationship from his point of view, her own innate honesty forced her to admit that Rayner had some justification for his behaviour. She tried to tell herself she was blameless, but not with much success. Guilt nagged at her. Not knowing he had been kept in gaol was no excuse. She should have found out what was happening to him, and tried to help, before leaving the country.

Lying awake herself at night, troubled and confused by her own problems, she was aware that Rayner quite often did not come upstairs until the light of dawn was visible. She never slept until she knew he was safely in bed, but she did not question why...

Marie stood in front of her father's painting, wondering for the umpteenth time why Rayner had kept it. Unconsciously she stroked her hand over her stomach. The mundane task of parenting could not have been easy for a man of Tom's talent.

She turned at the sound of the door opening, and without thought asked the usual question. 'How was Maisie tonight?'

Rayner's familiar features crumpled in such anguish, she wanted to rush and fold him in her arms. To comfort him.

'What happened?' she whispered, not daring to move.

He walked across the room and collapsed into the fireside chair, burying his head in his hands.

'Rayner.' Her heart squeezed in fear.

He lifted his haggard face, his grey eyes glittering strangely. 'Do you really care, or is it simply that your perfect manners demand you ask?' he rasped.

'That's not fair. Maisie means a lot to me.'

'Sorry, Marie, I have no cause to snap at you, but the news is not good. I spoke to the doctor tonight, and he's afraid Maisie is developing pneumonia, and at her age...' He flung his hands out in a helpless gesture.

Her eyes filled with moisture and she quickly blinked it away. She looked at Rayner, really looked at him for the first time in weeks. He had lost weight, his face was thinner, no longer tanned but sallow. Dark circles ringed his eyes, but even so his lean body possessed a powerful aura of controlled sensuality.

No...she cried inwardly as a vivid image of their lying in bed together naked, limbs intermingled, flashed in her mind. She cringed at her folly. What a time to reawaken to his potent brand of virility, when poor Maisie... She felt the colour rush to her face and in an effort to cover her confusion she said the first thing that came into her head.

'Why do you keep my father's painting when you hate him?'

'That.' Rayner stared at her, a puzzled look in his eyes. 'Because it is an excellent painting, and a last link with a girl I thought was dead,' he responded slowly. 'You're wrong, you know, Marie—I don't hate your father, though you obviously have a deep-seated problem in that direction.'

'Me?' she exclaimed in astonishment. She did not know what surprised her most, his linking her with the painting or his last comment.

'Yes, you, my dear,' he said quietly. 'I admit his outburst to the media hurt at the time, but now I can understand his reason and excuse him. If I had a seventeen-year-old daughter I loved as he loved you, and someone had taken her virginity, I might hit out at the man who had done it any way I could.'

'Since when were you an expert on my relationship with Tom?' she retorted angrily, ignoring the rest of his statement.

'Forget it, Marie,' he commanded bluntly. 'Get me something to eat—I'm going back to the hospital as soon as I've showered and changed.'

CHAPTER TEN

THE past week had been one long nightmare, forty-eight hours of it spent mostly at Maisie's bedside, watching the old lady gradually give up the fight for life.

It had given Marie too much time to think, and her thoughts had been far from comfortable. She had taken a long hard look at herself and she did not like what she saw.

Rayner had said their marriage would be a nine-day wonder, and he was right. Dozens of people had called in the past few weeks, with invitations to dine or parties, and very quickly any mention of Marie's and Rayner's earlier association had fizzled out. They had all, without exception, been sympathetic when the invitations had to be refused because of Maisie's illness.

Could Rayner also be right about her? Marie wondered. He had said she was prim, repressed, narrow-minded, and maybe she was, but her early life had made her that way. She had resented Tom, her father, but, looking back on her life with a new maturity, maybe she had misread her parents' characters.

True, they had travelled the country, but hadn't they always returned to Whitby? She always thought she had fought for her education, but they had never stopped her going to school. Other families had joined communes, but not her father. He was always too much of an individual, he had liked to fight for what he thought were just causes, but he had never forced his ideas on Marie. With the nature of a true artist he had had the power to detach himself from what was going on around him whenever he wanted to.

Was it possible she had taken his detachment as lack of caring? Rayner had said Tom loved her in his own way. Tom had given her all the freedom she could have wished for, but in her youth she had not realised what it meant. Instead she had allowed one word—'hippy'—to colour all her thinking. Now she found she could say the word without cringing. Surely that told her something.

She had judged her parents and found them wanting long before she was old enough to begin to understand them. She had never confided in them; it had taken the trauma of that midsummer night with Rayner before she had even admitted in plain words that she hated their lifestyle. Her mother had responded immediately, swallowing her own pride and taking Marie to her grandfather.

Wryly she admitted she had always blamed Tom for her mother's drug habit, but for all she knew her mother could have been taking drugs before she ever met Tom.

Finally she was forced to admit she had judged them too harshly. Across the world the Green Party was now a political force, and environmental issues were of the greatest concern to everyone. It was people like her parents, who had plugged away for three decades with what had seemed fanatical ideas, who were the pioneers of the now commonly held views of most intelligent people. Sadly she recognised that she would have liked the chance to know her parents as an adult. But she had a sneaking suspicion they would have found the woman she had become a disappointment.

Standing at the graveside with Rayner's arm around her shoulder, she thankfully accepted the snowy white handkerchief he pressed into her hand. She wiped her red and swollen eyes, and with a last look at the fresh mound of earth covered with dozens of beautiful floral tributes, she lifted her head.

'It's time to leave, Marie.'

Her eyes lingered on his gaunt features; the past week had been terrible for Rayner, and he looked so lonely, so vulnerable, her heart ached for him. His grey eyes glittered with a film of moisture, and she could feel the tension in his lean body as he turned her gently towards the waiting cars.

The last guest had left and Rayner was driving Ned and his wife home to their cottage. Wearily Marie set about collecting the last of the empty glasses the caterers had left and carried them through to the kitchen.

It felt odd to walk into the warm farmhouse-style room with its gleaming pine furniture and fittings, and know Maisie would never be here again. She had been so much a part of the place it looked empty without her.

She picked up the kettle, filled it at the tap and plugged it in. Maybe a cup of coffee would revive her, though she doubted it. She shivered, the emptiness of the big house closing in around her. While Maisie was ill, Bess from the village had stayed, but she had left after the funeral.

Marie took down a jar of instant coffee and mixed the granules in a cup of hot water. It was the first time she had been alone in the house, and the silence played on her over-taut nerves. Carrying the cup in one hand, she wandered through the hall to the drawing-room and collapsed on to the overstuffed sofa.

She drank the coffee in one go and, placing the cup on the floor—a bad habit, a thing she would never normally do—she wearily laid her head back and closed her eyes.

She needed to sleep, but that health-giving commodity had been denied her for the last few days. Her mind refused to rest; instead her head whirled with a confusion of thoughts and emotions she could not control. She told herself over and over again that she hated Rayner, but her avowals were beginning to sound weak even to her own ears. Seeing his care, his concern for Maisie, and watching him hurt like lesser mortals, melted the blessed numbness that had shielded her for so long, leaving her exposed and vulnerable.

She was on the defensive all the time. She could not help it. Her awareness of Rayner was such that it was agony for her to be in the same room with him. Marie sighed dejectedly. She knew she couldn't put off much longer making a decision on her future. With Maisie gone, she didn't think she could stay in this house on her own. The images of Rayner and Lisa in his London apartment would torment her mind. Imagination could be a liability as well as an asset, she concluded with a tired sigh, her eyelids drooping.

'Marie, we have to talk.'

Blinking, she opened her eyes, still half asleep. Rayner was sitting stiff-backed on the sofa beside her. She turned her head slightly to look at him. His silver hair was dishevelled, and the white shirt he was wearing with the dark suit was unbuttoned halfway down his chest, displaying a healthy amount of crisp, curling chest hair. A reminiscent smile of pleasure curved her lips as she remembered how it had felt to touch him there.

'Can't it wait? I'm tired,' she murmured softly. She was totally unaware of the seductive picture she presented. Her red hair framed her lovely face, tumbling in a riot of curls around her shoulders. Her full breasts jutted proudly against the soft black wool of her sweater dress as she arched her back and yawned widely. 'I'd rather go to bed.'

She heard his sharp intake of breath and her eyes widened in sudden alarm as he stared at her intently, his eyes burning on her body.

'Damn you, Marie, what are you trying to do to me?' he said hoarsely. He reached out one hand, and it fell lightly on her breast. 'Drive me out of my mind?'

He raised his eyes to hers, but she could not speak— all she could hear was the drumming of her heart beneath his hand.

'Do you want me to rape you, is that it? Is that to be my final punishment?' he said between his teeth, and then his hand tightened on her, his arm slid round her shoulders. 'The final irony, Marie,' he said hoarsely.

'Rayner?' she said anxiously. She had never seen him like this; his face was dark, twisted in pain.

'Yes, say my name.' His voice slurring, his mouth moved over hers.

He kissed her with an urgency that was breathtaking. A little voice of sanity said she should resist, but, closing her eyes, she tangled her fingers in his hair and kissed him back with all the pent-up hunger of weeks of abstinence. She clung to him, the blood pounding in her ears, and fire coursing through her veins.

Rayner raised his head, his breathing ragged. 'Oh, God, Marie, I need you so much, don't deny me, not tonight.' He groaned the words against her mouth. Then once more he was kissing her with a hungry desperation, his tongue finding every secret crevasse of her mouth.

Her own hunger matched his—feverishly she ran her hands over his broad chest, underneath his shirt. She stroked the muscular contours of his broad back, her nails digging into his flesh as she sought an even greater closeness. Her breasts were flattened beneath the heavy weight of him as he manoeuvred her lengthways on the sofa, his long body over hers, touching from head to toe.

For weeks they had existed in a curious limbo, the shadow of death hanging over them, and now it was as if they both needed to reaffirm the continuity of life, their own vitality.

In fumbling haste Rayner stripped her dress over her head and shed his own clothes. With scant appreciation for the preliminaries of lovemaking their bodies joined in a thrusting, primitive passion neither could control.

Marie had a fleeting, shocking image of her prim self paganly sprawled across the drawing-room sofa! But she didn't care.

She cried out as Rayner thrust deeper still, filling her body as he filled her heart and mind. She quivered on the brink of fulfilment, her slender legs locked round his waist, her hands digging into his shoulders as her body arched with intolerable tension. The wild pagan rhythm of their bodies moved as one in a final cataclysmic burst of energy. Convulsive shudders rocked her as Rayner's life force flowed into her, his great frame shaking uncontrollably.

'Marie, Marie, Marie,' he chanted her name in a guttural litany, the words torn from the depths of his throat as his sweat-soaked body collapsed against her.

She curled her arms around his neck and held him close, unable to speak, tears choked her throat and hazed her eyes, the force of emotion he aroused in her overwhelming her. She clung to him, glorying in his full weight upon her, the pounding beat of his heart and the deep rasping sound of his breathing the most captivating sound in the world.

She loved him, and with a bitter-sweet sadness she realised that it did not matter how he treated her or what his reasons were for marrying her. She wanted him and always would. Lying in his arms in total communion, satiated and at one, she knew she would accept anything she could from him.

If that meant sharing him with London, or whatever, so be it. They would have children—the thought of a blond-haired little boy to love was a great consolation. Half a loaf was better than none. God, she was thinking in clichés. Her love-swollen lips twitched in the beginnings of a smile that never materialised as Rayner swore violently and leapt off the sofa. He turned his back on her, pulling on his trousers with insulting haste.

'Rayner,' tentatively she whispered his name, 'what's wrong?'

'Wrong, wrong?' he exclaimed, and picking her clothes from the floor he dropped them on top of her. 'Get dressed,' he commanded. His grey eyes met hers and she glimpsed a flash of complete desolation in their silvery depths, before he looked away.

Trance-like, Marie slipped into her clothes. She had no idea what had happened, she did not understand his complete withdrawal. Was he regretting making love to her? The thought made her want to weep, but biting hard on her bottom lip she held back the question. She sat stiffly on the edge of the sofa, and glanced up at him. Some things it was better not to know, she thought with a sickening feeling of dread. His face was set in an expressionless mask. He was once more in complete control, as though the last half-hour had never been.

'Are you all right? Would you like a drink?' Rayner asked, avoiding her glance and walking across to where the drinks trolley stood. He poured a very large whisky into a crystal tumbler. There was something about the set of his broad shoulders, the stiffness of his usually lithe walk, that made Marie realise he was not so much in control as he wished to appear.

'I'm fine and no, thank you,' she said slowly, watching him as he turned and carefully walked to a chair a few feet away from the sofa. He sat down, and took a long swallow of the whisky.

'I'm sorry for what happened just now, Marie.' He drained the glass and put it down on the nearby table with a hand that trembled.

Marie's eyes widened in surprise. He actually looked nervous, and why was he apologising? She knew the feeling between them had been mutual. He could not have faked the tumultuous response. She had to believe that . . . 'I'm not,' she murmured, swallowing her pride and telling the truth.

His head shot up at her words and his grey eyes lingered on her flushed, wary face. 'You're too soft for your own good, Marie,' he opined wryly, 'and I don't deserve you. I know that now. I have for a long time.'

'I don't understand . . .' Was he trying to get rid of her with the oldest trick in the book? I don't deserve you. Was that supposed to make her feel good? Had her easy wanton response sickened him? A dozen questions spun in her brain, but she was unable to voice them.

'I'm not surprised,' Rayner responded, a wry smile twisting his sensuous mouth. 'I've had trouble understanding myself the past few months. But today I vowed on Maisie's grave I would put everything right. My treatment of you has been abominable, and I swore once the funeral was over you would have a full apology from me and your freedom. Instead I jumped on you like a sex-starved lunatic.' He snorted in self-disgust. 'They say the road to hell is paved with good intentions—in my case it should be ready-mixed concrete, I'm going to

Hades so fast,' he stated flatly, shaking his head in self-derision.

Marie's lips twitched at his twisted analogy, and a chuckle escaped her. 'Then I must be going with you, because I thoroughly enjoyed being jumped on by a sex-starved lunatic,' she responded, her golden eyes lit with laughter, all her much vaunted cool reserve dissolving as for once she allowed her true nature to surface.

His silver-blond hair lay in a rumpled mass across his forehead, as he uncharacteristically combed his fingers through it. His grey eyes glittered strangely in his gaunt face when he lifted his head and met her gaze, but he did not seem to register her words as he continued in the same flat, toneless voice. 'You're not making this easy for me, and I can't say I blame you after the way I've behaved. But I have talked it over with a priest and there is a possibility of an annulment. If a marriage is entered into with deceit or for the wrong reason it can be arranged.'

'But...' It all sounded so cut and dried—for Rayner to have actually enquired into the prospect of petitioning the Pope so stunned Marie she could only stare at him in horror. Did he really want to get rid of her that badly? Nothing it seemed would ever deaden the pain inside her. She fought to control the trembling in her limbs, and blinked back the moisture from her golden eyes. There was no longer just herself to think about...

'I don't want my freedom, Rayner,' she informed him quietly, inwardly quaking. 'I want to stay here.' Her mouth felt dry as a desert, and she swallowed nervously. She had told the truth, she could do no more. The next move was up to Rayner. She raised her eyes, a silent plea in their topaz depths, but it was lost on Rayner—he stared fixedly beyond her into the dark corner of the room.

'You need have no worries about returning to France. I will personally explain to Henri it was all my fault.' He continued speaking as if he had not heard her. 'I know how bitterly you regret our marriage, but if it's any consolation I'm hurting more than I thought it possible to feel and survive.'

'Rayner,' she whispered his name, the torment in his eyes giving her the first glimmer of hope. 'I said I do not want to leave.'

'Not want...' He stared at her with an incredulous look on his face, quickly controlled. Her words had finally registered, and with fast-pounding heart she bravely withstood the probing intensity of his gaze. 'You want to stay here——' he hesitated, a nerve twitching in his jaw '—with me?'

'Yes, if you still want me—that is...' she qualified hesitantly.

An agonising silence ensued, making Marie feel as if she were hovering on the edge of a precipice. A derisive smile curved his firm lips, and her heart sank.

'Want you? God, Marie, that's a poor word for the way I feel about you.' In two strides he crossed the space dividing them, and sank down beside her on the sofa, but careful not to touch her. 'I love you, I think I always have.'

Marie caught her breath, incredulous joy flowing through her—but there had been too much between them for her to believe him. 'But on our wedding night——'

'I was insanely jealous,' he muttered quickly.

'Jealous?' It didn't make sense. 'But your stay in prison... You blamed me.' She was incapable of understanding his reasoning.

'Please, Marie, let me explain.' He reached for her hand and curved his long fingers around it. 'I never really blamed you for my stay in prison. I loved you and I was confused and hurting because I had tried to ask you to marry me, and I couldn't believe your reaction. I was little more than a virgin myself at the time, and eventually I concluded that as a lover I must have been lousy.'

'Oh, no!'

Rayner did not seem to hear her gasp. 'With hindsight, I know now, it was an unfortunate set of circumstances that kept me in gaol. But I did hit the policeman, more than once. I would probably have got the same sentence even if you had come forward and explained the situation.'

'But you told me——' she began—she had not forgotten his disparaging remarks or his coldness.

'I said a lot of things on our wedding night I bitterly regretted the next day, but you have to understand, Marie. Grief does strange things to a man. I should know better than most. I thought you were dead, I cried— God, how I cried—and then I grew angry. I'm not proud at the way I have behaved the last few years, but at last I can see the reasons more clearly. When I saw you in Deauville, I was even angrier...' He smiled with wry self-mockery. 'I know this will sound terrible, but I was furious that you were alive and looking so stunningly beautiful and obviously happy and successful. I felt cheated in some way.'

'Oh, Rayner.' Moisture glazed her eyes; she could not doubt the sincerity of his words.

'I've been through a hell of a time trying to sort myself out, Marie. But I want you to know, even back then, when I had to return here because of my father's illness, I think I knew that I loved you. I promised my father I would marry, but I also told him it was you I intended to marry. I even told Maisie...'

Marie remembered that the first day she'd arrived Maisie had told her that Rayner loved her, but she had not believed the older woman. A tear sparkled on her thick lashes before spilling softly down her cheek. So much misunderstanding.

'The rest you know. I met you, wanted you, and asked you again to marry me. I confess I didn't admit to myself I loved you; I think I was still rocking from the death of my father. Or perhaps it was my protection against being hurt again. I don't know. I only know that when you walked down that church aisle, looking so incredibly beautiful, I knew I meant every word of the vows I made. When we got to Paris and the hotel I was a mass of nerves. I could barely speak civilly, and later—my God! I couldn't even wait to have a shower, I wanted you so badly,' he groaned, and reaching out his free hand he brushed the tear from her cheek.

Marie stared into his warm grey eyes, and what she saw there made her heart expand in her breast till she thought it would burst. They were both remembering the passionate, uninhibited lovemaking. 'Then why did you turn on me?' she asked, not bothering to hide her bewilderment.

Rayner dropped his eyes, and clasping both her hands in his he studied them as though his life depended on it. She watched in amazement as a dull red flush spread up over his face. She had never seen Rayner blush before. 'Why, Rayner?' she reiterated.

'Pure male chauvinism—I was stupidly, irrationally jealous. You gave me everything that night, and afterwards all I could think of was where you had learnt to make love like that. Certainly not from me. I hated the idea of you with any other man. Then, when you said it was better than the first time, you scored a direct hit on my male ego. It seemed to confirm my former youthful conclusion that as a lover I had been a disappointment to you. I lashed out at you with all the anger and resentment I had nursed for years, and I hated myself for it. But I just couldn't seem to stop.' He lifted his head, a shamefaced grin curving his firm mouth.

'You were never a disappointment, Rayner—the first time was marvellous, you were so tender, so caring, it was only the word "hippy". I was young and far too sensitive—you must believe me.' And the truth was there for him to read in her wide golden eyes. 'There was never any other man, only you...'

'You let me think there was,' he shot back with a flash of his old arrogance. Then wryly he added, 'But after the party when you told me what you thought of me, and let slip there had been no one else all those years, I was pole-axed. By dragging out all the old garbage from the past, to hide my jealousy, I had ruined our relationship.'

'It was my only defence against you, I told you I loved you, and——'

'No, don't say it, Marie, I don't need you reminding me what a complete and utter idiot I've been. By the day of the party I finally admitted to myself I loved you, and finding you in the woods made everything perfect. I was happy and so sure we could start again that when Lisa cast her poison it never even occurred to me you would be hurt by it.'

Marie had forgotten about the other woman, but now her early fear returned in force. 'She was your mistress, and I hated the thought of your discussing me with her.'

'I told you the truth about Lisa—we had a brief affair and it was over long before I met you again. But I have since discovered how she found out. Jake told her. He was the journalist whom I asked to track you down when I had to return to be with my father.'

Suddenly everything made sense to Marie, and happiness, sharp and sweet, surged through her. 'Poor Jake,' she murmured, and she could understand the other man's pain. Hadn't he told her himself he loved Lisa?

'Poor Jake, my eye,' Raynet exclaimed, and pulling her into his arms he said, 'It's your poor husband who needs your sympathy. This poor demented man who is begging your forgiveness, and praying you will stay with him.'

Marie curled up on his lap and wound her slender arms around his neck. They had lots to sort out, but she had the joyous feeling they would have a lifetime to do it in.

'Can you forgive me, Marie?' he asked seriously, leaning his head back to look down into her lovely face, an oddly vulnerable expression in his grey eyes.

'Well, if I can climb down from my ivory...' she began in a teasing tone, but stopped at the flash of pain she glimpsed in his gaze. 'Yes, my darling Rayner, I can forgive you anything, just so long as you hold me in your arms and allow me to love you.' Then sombrely she asked, 'But can you forget my unconscious betrayal? And forgive me, because I do love you so very, very much,' she freely admitted.

'You have nothing to reproach yourself with, Marie darling. I've been a damned fool—I love you and I always will,' he groaned, and lowering his head took possession of her lips in a long, tender, searching kiss that proclaimed his love as clearly as words.

'A fine baby boy, nine pounds, delivered at four a.m. on midsummer's morning. What are you going to call him? "Bottom"?' The doctor burst out laughing at his own joke, and gently laid the baby in his mother's arms.

Marie looked at the tiny baby in her arms, and then up at her husband, a huge smile wreathing her lovely but tired face. 'He's perfect, Rayner.'

'He could not be anything else with you as his mother, my darling.' And, leaning over the hospital bed, he planted a soft kiss on her damp forehead. 'I love you, Marie.' Then he bestowed another one on the top of his son's head.

Marie sighed her contentment; the last few months had been full of laughter and love, more than she had believed possible. She looked at Rayner—he was standing by the bed, tall and broad-shouldered, his chest puffed out with pride, the epitome of the new father.

'The last few months have been like a midsummer night's dream,' she told him quietly. 'I do love you.'

'And I love you, my darling, more than I can ever tell you. But I'm not calling my son Bottom for anyone,' he chuckled.

'But it is a coincidence, his being born at the summer solstice. How about Merlin?'

'No way,' Rayner growled in mock anger. 'We were crazy enough one midsummer's night to get caught *in flagrante delicto*. It was my own fault—I should have known better than to play around with a half-French girl. He'll have a good Anglo-Saxon name. Something like Eldred might be useful.'

'Eldred.' Marie rolled the name around her tongue. 'I'm not sure I care for that, Rayner.' She looked at the sleeping baby, and back up to her husband. His grey eyes were gleaming with laughter.

'What does it mean?' she asked, her full lips parting in a smile in response to Rayner's obvious amusement, but her lovely eyes had a slightly wary gleam—the last few months had taught her that this husband of hers had a wicked sense of humour.

'It means Old Counsel. Very appropriate, I think. Just in case his sexy mother leads me astray again and I need one.' And throwing his head back he laughed out loud at the blushing indignation on Marie's face.

my VALENTINE 1992

Celebrate the most romantic day of the year with
MY VALENTINE 1992—a sexy new collection of four
romantic stories written by our famous Temptation
authors:

> GINA WILKINS
> KRISTINE ROLOFSON
> JOANN ROSS
> VICKI LEWIS THOMPSON

My Valentine 1992—an exquisite escape into a romantic
and sensuous world.

 Harlequin Books

VAL-92-R

Take 4 bestselling love stories FREE

Plus get a FREE surprise gift!

Special Limited-time Offer

Mail to Harlequin Reader Service®

In the U.S.
3010 Walden Avenue
P.O. Box 1867
Buffalo, N.Y. 14269-1867

In Canada
P.O. Box 609
Fort Erie, Ontario
L2A 5X3

YES! Please send me 4 free Harlequin Presents® novels and my free surprise gift. Then send me 6 brand-new novels every month, which I will receive months before they appear in bookstores. Bill me at the low price of $2.49* each—a savings of 30¢ apiece off cover prices. There are no shipping, handling or other hidden costs. I understand that accepting the books and gift places me under no obligation ever to buy any books. I can always return a shipment and cancel at any time. Even if I never buy another book from Harlequin, the 4 free books and the surprise gift are mine to keep forever.

*Offer slightly different in Canada—$2.49 per book plus 69¢ per shipment for delivery. Canadian residents add applicable federal and provincial sales tax. Sales tax applicable in N.Y.

106 BPA ADLZ

306 BPA ADMF

Name	(PLEASE PRINT)	
Address		Apt. No.
City	State/Prov.	Zip/Postal Code

This offer is limited to one order per household and not valid to present Harlequin Presents® subscribers. Terms and prices are subject to change.

PRES-91

© 1990 Harlequin Enterprises Limited